STRIKING OUT

THE CEMETERY DIARIES

JAN TOOLAN

Prologue

Everyone knows a cemetery is no place to be when darkness falls. I certainly knew better, having been warned no fewer than eight billion times by my mother. But then she's a worrier, and being twelve meant I knew pretty much everything, so nothing was off limits in my world, unless you count broccoli and liver. I had passed through the cemetery plenty of times in broad daylight, as it was the most convenient route between my house and just about everywhere else. The gnarled old trees and crooked stones had proven harmless on these sojourns, and the place could be positively peaceful under a blanket of fresh sparkling snow. I'm not sure who my mother thought might be lurking behind the headstones; who in their right mind hangs out with deadbeats? Okay, bad joke, but seriously, not once had I encountered a single shake, shiver, or shadow as I threaded my way amongst the granite and marble and occasional plastic geranium.

Actually, it was kind of intriguing and every time I altered my route, I'd see something I'd missed before.

Sometimes it was a new name on a stone, or an old sepia photo of a woman from the Old Country. And then there was always a new body popping up. Well, not literally because that **would** be terrifying, but a fresh mound of dirt always meant a new soul had joined others long since passed, the most recent addition being my own grandmother. Personally, I thought she deserved one of those cool crypts, the ones with doors and windows where the bodies go inside instead of in the ground. But my parents claimed nobody did that anymore, and besides, it was too expensive. You'd think that since my father was the caretaker of these rolling acres he could have pulled some strings or cut some kind of a deal, but in the ground she went.

So, when it came to cemeteries, and this one in particular, I was fearless. That is until one spring evening, when the snows had finally melted and the last dead leaves were skittering along the ground even as new buds formed in their vacant perches. I won't say my mother was right, because I'm twelve and that rarely happens, but what happened that night was the most frightening and fascinating thing that has ever happened to me.

Actually, there were two of us who could tell the story, but neither of us wanted to be the laughingstock of the school cafeteria. Nobody would have believed us anyway, but just to be safe we took a solemn vow. Linking arms as we sat atop the oldest stone, we swore to never, ever, as long as we lived, cross our hearts and hope to die, stick a needle in our eye, tell another living, breathing soul about what happened that night at Shady Lawn.

Until now…

Chapter 1

I wanted to die. Okay, maybe not; but if the ground had opened up and swallowed me whole at that moment, I wouldn't have gone down swinging. I'd have been far better off among the earthworms and slugs than listening to the taunts of my team mates and seeing the sad, slow, shake of my coach's hanging head.

It was my fault; I had blown the golden opportunity. All I had to do was step up to the plate, stare down Goony Graves, and knock the ball out of the park. It was the bottom of the ninth, two out, two on, and everybody knew Goony was the worst pitcher in the league.

"No sweat", I thought as I sauntered up to the plate. "So the game is tied and you're the last hope" went the voice in my head. "Been there, done that", I murmured confidently as I tapped my bat on home plate.

I lifted the bat above my shoulder and planted my feet to await the pitch that would have my team shrieking for joy.

Whoooosh.

"Steeeeeerike one!" screamed the umpire.

I heard some of my buddies groan, and I have to admit, I was pretty baffled myself. I had actually let one of Goony's pitches sail right across the plate! It was time to get serious. I stared Goony down as I set my sites on the white orb and actually knocked the next pitch high into the air, right into foul territory. Luckily Spike Stone, the first baseman, wasn't exactly quick or he would have caught it and that would have been that.

"Another chance, just one more chance" whispered that voice in my head.

Unfortunately, that little voice wasn't sounding too confident, and I didn't need that pressure just now.

"No problem", I answered with more bravado than I actually felt, "bring it on, Goony!"

Goony dug his foot into the dirt, hunkered down, and stared fiercely into my eyes.

The catcher was in position, ready to finalize my humiliation. Well, there was no way I'd give him the satisfaction. The crowd had gone silent. The beat of my own heart slamming in my chest rumbled like thunder.

I planted my foot and lifted my bat one more time, preparing myself for the roar of the crowd. The ball came hurtling toward me with a little wobble so typical of Goony as I brought my bat around.

"Thwack!"

"STEEEEEEEEERIKE THREE!" bellowed the ecstatic umpire. I say ecstatic because he also happened to be Goony's uncle. The horrible sound the ball made as it smacked into the catcher's glove made me cringe.

Then the crowd erupted alright, but it wasn't my crowd. As I stood there in stunned silence, I saw the hanging heads of every team mate, every parent and grandparent, and never had I felt so alone and small in my life. The unthinkable had happened and all I could do was watch as Goony and Spike embraced, which was no easy feat since Goony looked more like a Sumo wrestler than a pitcher. At least that made it impossible for him to be lofted high upon the shoulders of his team mates, a scene I had pictured being played out with me riding high as I was jostled toward the cheering crowd. This was the first game of the season, and my vision of a perfect season was ruined.

Not until the field had finally cleared and the dugout was nearly empty did I slowly trudge out of the batter's box and off the field, with that sickening "thwack" reverberating through my brain. The only one left waiting on the bench was my friend Marley, who also happened to be one amazing shortstop. Maybe because she was my friend, or maybe just because she was a girl and they were almost always nicer than boys, she patted me on the back and threw her arm around my shoulder.

"It's okay Jake. It's only the first game of the season. There are plenty of games left to get ol' Goony back," Marley consoled. "Besides, that was one of the craziest pitches I've ever seen the Goon Man throw. Even he was surprised when you missed it! What amazes me even more is that Taylor Tooms wasn't shaking too hard to catch that strike in the first place. He's not used to people striking out."

"Thanks for that reminder, Mar! We all know I shoulda knocked that first one right over Goony's fat head! I must be rusty from not playing all winter long. Good thing it's Friday so I don't have to face all these guys at school tomorrow. The humiliation would be too much to bear. It will be pretty hard to avoid Coach all weekend since he lives conveniently right next door. He'll be storming into the kitchen bright and early in the morning to haul me off to the batting cages. I'm sure he'll have a nice easy practice in mind, with like 100 balls or so whizzing toward me at 80 miles per hour. I'll be lucky to ever lift a bat again when we're done. He and Pop are probably planning strategy as I speak!"

My shoulders slumped and my head hung so low that the earthworms could've hopped on for a ride. Luckily, Marley offered no further consolation, knowing me well enough to realize that there were no words that could eradicate the hideous moment I had just experienced.

We packed up our gloves and bats and slowly headed out of the park. Even my parents had already headed for home, a sure sign that I'd be getting a full game analysis from my pop when I caught up with them. I walked even slower and refused Marley's offer of ice cream as we passed the *Scooper's* Ice Cream truck in the parking lot. Instead of the ding-ding of the bell that always brought kids running to the pink and white striped truck, all I heard was the "thwack, thwack" of the ball smacking into Taylor Tooms' glove.

I swear, even the horses in the carousel were braying and laughing at my utter devastation as we passed by. I turned around and looked in the window at all the little kids, grinning as they went 'round and 'round, up and down on their pastel ponies. I almost wished they'd break loose from their shiny brass poles and trample me. The corny calliope music curdled my brain, and visions of Goony grinning fiendishly from atop a magenta mare danced before my eyes.

"Who cares; go ahead and laugh, you stupid painted horses!" I yelled angrily, raising my bat above my head. "I'm too old to care about riding you when all you do is run in circles anyway! What do you know about baseball?"

Mar grabbed me by the arm and propelled me away from the scene of my outburst. Maybe she thought I was going to bust into the carousel and take a swing at a stallion or two. I had more sense than to become tomorrow's headline in the *Marble Times*, but then again there's no telling what I'd have done with that vision of Goony taunting me.

"Thanks, Mar. I lost it for a minute there," I said sheepishly. "The last thing I need is to become a spectacle on the sidewalk with a bunch of angry moms forming a posse to hunt me down for scaring their little darlings. I've had enough for one night."

We left the park and crossed the street just as the streetlights awakened from their daytime slumber. There was nothing in the world that could make me feel better and lift me from despair right now. Well, on second thought, my grandma's famous chocolate chip cookies might. But then I remembered that she had died during the last big snow storm in February and, with her, my last hope of salvaging anything but gloom and misery.

Chapter 2

We walked on together for a few minutes, the silence doing more to quiet me than any words Marley might have offered to comfort me. No doubt she was thinking about her own missed play earlier in the game that allowed the tying run to score in the first place. But all anybody will remember is that I struck out in the clutch, against Goony of all people! It was too much to bear, and right now I wished home was a million miles away. Pop would be sitting at the kitchen table, ready to launch into a play-by-play of the entire game, and I was in no mood to dredge up the nightmare I had just endured. Mom would be puttering around, trying to say nice things intended to make my debacle seem trivial, but failing miserably. Even her chocolate chip cookies, soft and flat, wouldn't do the trick. For some reason, she could never get that magical combination of crispy outside, chewy inside, grandma cookies. How she missed that lesson from her own mother I'll never know. Now it was too late…forever.

Too soon we came upon the iron gates leading into Shady Lawn. This was the shortcut back to Marble Manor, with its tree-lined streets laid out like a perfect grid. Where every lawn was neatly mown and edged, and an army of bobbing yellow daffodils stood at attention along the front walks as spring marched in again. But now dusk was falling and the daffodils would be nodding their heads as shadows crept across the yards. Inside, lights would be glowing warmly, hinting at scenes of families returning home to watch TV while they scooped their way through luscious ice cream sundaes or crunched on warm, buttery popcorn. I wished right then that I lived in Nebraska, a nice easy walk of about 800 miles or so. I would even have settled for a mountain of homework as a means of escaping the game analysis, but it was Friday and there was not even a project due that could provide me with an excuse.

As Marley started through the twelve foot high, black, wrought iron gates, thrown open as if knowing there was no need to keep the inhabitants from escaping, I hesitated.

"Mar, hold up," I said. "Why don't we take the long way home?"

"Don't even tell me you're afraid to walk through the cemetery, Jake Diggs!" exclaimed Marley. "We've walked through this place hundreds of times!"

"Geez, Mar, you know me better than that! Remember the first time we walked through here and you were ready to pee your pants the whole time?" I reminded her rather cruelly.

"Alright, wise guy, I was seven years old and you set me up! It wasn't the cemetery that scared me; it was the rest of the kids popping up from behind the stones that freaked me out. Anyway, that's ancient history!" Marley retorted. More gently she asked, "But, what gives?", still willing to give me a break apparently.

"It's just that I'm in no hurry to get home tonight, ya know?" I replied forlornly, scuffing my feet on the blacktop.

"Yeah, I know, but it wasn't entirely your fault, remember. If I hadn't missed that line drive the tying run never would have scored in the first place! "Besides", Marley pointed out reasonably, "it'll take another half an hour if we go the long way, and I don't want to miss my favorite show, *Crypt Raiders.*"

So much for all that friendly sympathy, I thought. With a heavy shrug of my sagging shoulders, I relented.

"Okay, in we go," I said and trudged through the gate.

We began the slow climb up the main road, past the small stone chapel erected on a grassy circle that split the road. That chapel always reminded me of a miniature castle and was often the setting when we played in Shady Lawn. I guess when your dad is in charge of the place it loses some of its mystery. We were smart enough to avoid such antics on big visiting days like Memorial Day, Mother's Day, and Father's Day, though. Somehow the relatives didn't much care for the idea of a bunch of kids tearing across the heads and feet of their family members. I pointed out to my pop that since they were dead they couldn't feel our tramping feet or hear our shrieks, but he told me it was about showing respect and advised me not to get carried away when visitors were around. It still made no sense to me and the other kids that we had to pretend we were in church in a place where the souls were beyond the saving words of any sermon. I have to admit, though, that the thought of kids clambering over my own grandmother's grave was pretty annoying, so I kind of saw pop's point now. We were beyond such childish games now anyway.

Marley was sporting a slight grin, apparently lost in similar memories of when we used to come here with other neighborhood kids, making up elaborate tales of knights and battles and fair maidens as we darted amongst the stones and crypts. Marley wasn't exactly your fair maiden type, but since she was the only girl, she was stuck with the role.

Just remembering our silly games made me feel a little better, and I felt a smile playing at the corners of my mouth.

Darting behind a tall stone, Marley peeked out, inquiring, "Sir Jake of Marble, have you come to slay the fierce dragon?"

"Aye, fair maiden, I have my trusty bat here and I shall save thee from its fiery clutches!" I exclaimed. I began swinging my bat at the imaginary foe, and then strode to the nearest stone, a large four-header, climbing on top of it.

"Give me your hand, fair maiden, and I shall whisk you away upon my noble steed to my own castle, far grander than this heap, and we shall live happily ever after," was my response as I bowed deeply in her direction

Marley let loose in a fit of giggles and before I knew it, the sound of my own laughter joined hers, breaking the silence of the deeply slumbering souls surrounding us. But enough silly kid games; it was getting darker and we needed to get moving. As we crested the hill, I turned right, instead of left, which had Marley wondering what I was up to now.

"I just want to stop and see my grandma while we're here," I explained. She's just a few rows over and we'll only stay a minute," I promised.

Now, neither of us was afraid, you understand, but dusk was quickly becoming dark and we would have a hard time finding our way home. It turns out there's no need for lights along the streets of the dearly departed; their cars had been parked long ago.

I led the way to the mound of earth that marked my grandmother's place, and we sat atop the stone bearing the names of her and my grandfather. The withered petals of chrysanthemums, daisies, and gladioli had long since blown away. Soon the mound would settle as the spring thaw proceeded and my father or one of his workers would level it out and plant grass seed to cover her. But for now we rested our cleats on the rocky mound and sat in silence. I swear I caught the faint scent of crisp-chewy chocolate chip cookies, warm from the oven, wafting around us in the cool evening air. Perhaps it was just my imagination, or maybe I really could smell the delicious scent coming from the cookie I slipped into grandma's casket when I said my last good-bye. Whatever the reason, I silently talked to her about the game and told her my sad story. By the time I finished, the sweet scent was fading back into memory, but I felt better.

"Let's roll'" said Marley. "It's going to get dark soon and we don't want to be wandering around here like ghosts all night."

"You're right, as usual Mar," I conceded. "Let's roll."

As we picked up our gear and found our way back to the road, the wind picked up, scattering the dry, dead leaves upward into mini tornados. A few big rain drops plopped on the ground, sounding like bombs going off where they hit the paved road. A cloudburst was about to drench us but good, and there was no way we'd make it home before we were soaked and shivering from the sudden spring storm.

"Come on!" I yelled as the noise grew around us. "In here, quick!"

Marley didn't ask questions, a rare moment for her, but followed me as I ran. I swung open the door of a nearby crypt, which startled Marley, but she held her tongue until we were safely inside. The noise had been deafening outside as thunder clapped and the wind howled, but inside the cacophony was muffled enough to carry on a conversation. I knew this was exactly what Marley had in mind and she didn't disappoint me.

"Jake!" she shrieked, "What are we doing in this, this, this dead house? Get me out of here this second or I'm going to scream!"

"Well, if you want my opinion, you already ARE screaming, Mar," I calmly replied. "Relax; you know you can trust me!"

Thankfully she took a deeeeeeeeeeeep breath, looked me right in the eyes, and opened her mouth to speak.

"AAAAAAAAAAAAHHHHHHHHHHHHHHHH
HHHH!"

Her scream shattered the night, rivaling the tumult outside the crypt, reverberating in my tortured eardrums. I grabbed her hard by the shoulders and gave her a rough shake.

"MAR!" I shouted. "KNOCK IT OFF! YOU'RE OKAY!"

Though there was terror in her eyes, she clamped her mouth shut and just sat there, shaking uncontrollably. I was beginning to think it would have been better to be drenched than to be sitting here in this musty cavern with my best friend looking like she'd never speak to me again once we got out of here. Although we'd explored these acres countless times before, we'd never actually entered a dead house. Even I had to admit it was a little spooky, especially with the sound and light show building outside.

I quietly and calmly explained to her where we were and reassured her that once the rain slowed we'd make a beeline for home. This seemed to do the trick as her breathing returned to normal and the shaking settled into occasional tremors.

"Mar," I said slowly, "we are just sitting in this little house waiting for the rain to stop. There is nothing to be afraid of, there is nobody here but us, and we'll be gone before you know it."

Finally, Marley found her voice, small though it was, and tried to explain her reaction. "It's not who's in here that I'm afraid of. I've been claustrophobic ever since my brother locked me in the hall closet with his pet gerbil when I was four years old. I can't stand to be cooped up in small spaces."

"Well, the door isn't locked and as far as I know, there aren't any gerbils here.

The one rabbit I did see headed for the hills as soon as you screamed, though."

Marley punched me, hard, in the shoulder, but I was willing to be her punching bag if it kept her from thinking about our predicament. I rubbed the sting away and as the rain pinged on the tarnished copper roof above, we began to take our first look around. Since we were stuck in here for now, our curiosity finally got the best of us and we figured we might as well explore the place. As luck would have it there were a couple of those tall white candles in red glass holders flanking each side of a small marble bench set beneath the stained glass window on the back wall. Astonishingly, they were actually lit! We didn't stop to think who might have done that, but picked them up instead, holding them out in front of us.

We stuck together as we walked slowly down one side of the crypt, holding the candles so we could read the inscriptions in the walls. There were two names, one in the top section, and one in the section below. Apparently, we had discovered the inner sanctum and final resting place of Jonas Parker and his wife Johanna. We turned to face the other side, holding the candles aloft once again, and introduced ourselves to two more members of the Parker family, Harold and Genevieve, their children. That pretty much ended our investigation in the tiny space, so we sat side by side on the small bench, discussing our findings.

"Whoever takes care of the Parkers does a pretty good job." I said. "There are no broken windows, the door isn't hanging off its hinges, and there don't seem to be any animals living here. No spider webs, dead leaves… nothing. Besides, somebody must keep these candles going."

"Wouldn't that be your father or one of his workers, Jake?" asked Marley, ever the logical one.

"No, I'm pretty sure that it has to be a friend or family member. The cemetery staff doesn't take care of upkeep like painting, cleaning, or candles; nothing beyond the usual landscape stuff." I replied. "Sometimes volunteers form the historical society will tidy things up, especially if it's the grave of some old big deal from back in the day. I'll have to ask my dad; I'm sure he knows something about it."

Outside the fury of the storm seemed to be subsiding and Marley and I discussed the possibility of making a break for home. We decided to keep one candle with us, just in case, and return it tomorrow. Surely nobody would be stopping here between now and then and notice it was missing, we reasoned. As Marley held her candle, I placed mine back on the floor in the small space between the bench and Genevieve Parker. A small, whitish flash caught my eye and I looked back to where I had placed the candle, worried that perhaps I had tipped it when I set it down.

Oddly out of place in the otherwise pristinely clean interior of the crypt, I bent to gingerly pick up the scrap of paper that had caught my eye. It appeared to be very old; not the white lined paper we had in school, but yellowed and stiff. Mar and I had once used tea bags to stain paper for a history project, and it reminded me of this paper in my hand.

Marley had been near the door, one hand outstretched to push her way out when she realized I was no longer right behind her. She turned to see what was keeping me.

"Yo, Diggs, you coming or what?" she asked impatiently. "It's getting dark and the rain has slowed so let's move it."

She spotted the object in my hand and couldn't resist joining me to investigate its contents. Slowly I opened the crumpled paper, which crackled in protest. I felt Marley shudder beside me and that's when it happened.

The crypt suddenly filled with a blinding light and the door blew open. The shrieking wind swirled and moaned, whipping leaves and debris in around us. I felt myself lifted from my feet and saw Marley had been as well. The two of us swirled around and around, higher and higher in this impossibly small space, like two ghosts in a macabre dance. I linked my arm through hers, afraid we'd be torn apart by the tornado that gripped us.

The next thing I knew we had crashed back to the ground and the world went black.

Chapter 3

"Jake! Jake! Wake up!" came Marley's urgent whisper in my ear, accompanied by some pretty fierce shoves to my shoulder.

She sounded far away but her shoving told me she was right next to me as I slowly opened my eyes. My body felt like I'd been hit by a train and I let out a groan as I tried to sit up.

"Where are we?" I asked from my fog.

"I have no idea, but I have a feeling we're not in Kansas anymore." came Marley's pithy reply.

"Kansas? We don't live in Kansas. Why would we be in Kansas?" I asked, still groggy from whatever had just happened to us.

"Jake, sometimes you are soooooooo dense." said Marley, shaking her head and rolling her eyes at me.

I rubbed my eyes, rolled my shoulders, and tried to make sense of the strange surroundings. The last thing I remembered was picking up that piece of paper in the crypt at Shady Lawn. I could tell that we weren't inside that crypt now, but what I couldn't figure out was exactly **where** we were.

Slowly we rose to our feet and began to explore the tiny building we were in. It was a little bigger than the crypt, and although I didn't see or smell any evidence of dead bodies, who knew what was beneath the dirt floor as we scuffed along. The walls were constructed of wide, rough wooden boards, topped with a peaked roof. Because it was dark it was difficult to see much more than those few insignificant details.

"It looks like some sort of shed." I deducted. "It's too small to be a garage and it doesn't smell like cars."

"Great job, Sherlock! Now maybe you can figure out WHY we're in a shed instead of a crypt and HOW we're supposed to get home!" Marley's attempt at sarcasm fell short, the squeak in her voice giving away her fear.

Judging from that familiar squeaky tone, I was thinking Mar might soon be in need of another intervention to avoid launching into full hysteria. I knew I'd better come up with something fast.

"Okay, calm down Mar, and grab that candle. Maybe if we find that piece of paper it will give us some clue about what happened and we'll figure out what to do next." I instructed, thinking that if I kept her busy I could save my eardrums in the deal. I didn't think I should point out that the presence of the candle was most peculiar. There were enough unanswered questions for now without delving into more of the unexplained.

Marley picked the candle up from the floor and carefully extracted it from the red stained-glass holder so we'd have better lighting to work with. I wasn't so sure this was such a good idea because now the contents of the shed danced eerily in the flickering candlelight, and Marley wasn't looking too thrilled. She cast a worried glance around at the crazily dancing shadows as I readied my fingers in plug position.

A few seconds went by and no sound split the night, so I opened my eyes and looked at the ground, figuring she must have passed out. But no, to my enormous relief, there stood the same Marley I knew on the baseball field, brave and gritty, intently scanning our surroundings.

After letting go of the breath I'd been unconsciously holding, I began to look around as well.

"Get your fingers out of your ears, Jake. I might be a girl but I'm not a princess." Marley replied with her famous roll of the eyes. "What do you think this place is?" she asked.

It was time to sport the wisdom of my twelve years, an opportunity to demonstrate my vast knowledge of all things and flex my impressive brain power. I puffed up my chest and gave her my best educated guess.

"I have absolutely no idea."

There was some sort of table along the back wall, a work bench perhaps. A few pieces of broken furniture were stacked in one corner; a chair with three legs, and an old cradle that no longer rocked. Above us, hanging from heavy nails hammered into the walls, was an odd assortment of stuff so old-fashioned that we couldn't even name much, other than some rope and some metal tools. There were a few other odds and ends arranged on the floor along the walls, but, altogether, none of it gave us a sense of what went on in here.

"Maybe it's a workshop, or one of those out buildings like on a farm where they keep stuff for fixing fences and things." reasoned Marley.

"Or maybe it's a torture chamber and we're the next victims!" I leered in my best Dracula accent. The fact that I was now holding the candle directly below my chin made me look even more fiendish, or so I thought proudly.

"Boys!" exclaimed Marley impatiently, crossing her arms over her chest, ignoring my rather impressive imitation.

"Well, Professor Marley," I answered peevishly, "we're never going to figure anything out if we don't look at that piece of paper that landed us here in the first place." I was miffed; the least she could have done was acknowledge my amazing acting skills.

Marley looked back to where I had recently been prone on the floor and, reaching with tentative fingers, picked the paper up and placed it on the rickety workbench. Slowly she smoothed the paper out, being careful not to tear the fragile parchment.

"It looks like a page from somebody's diary." Marley said dreamily as she gazed at the flowing handwriting.

"Let's set the candle down next to it so we can read what it says. Hopefully there's some clue in there that will help us figure out what's going on, because right now even my mom's soft, flat cookies are starting to sound really good."

July 19, 1619

Dear Diary,

Papa has locked me in the shed once again. He is so busy with his comings and goings he scarcely has time to bother with me. I'm so lonely since mama passed, is it any wonder that I escape from that dreary house to find amusement? Never did I imagine when I crept out the front door last night that papa would come looking for me in my bedroom, expecting to find me sewing or working at my lessons. But to my surprise, he was right there waiting in the parlor when I returned, and now here I've been all this long, lonely night. I fear he may keep me here for a fortnight or more, so severe was his rage at my deception. Alas, I am left to wallow in my sorrows and, in my own anger, I swear I shall keep to myself whatever I have learned. I am tormented, knowing that my secret could save all within the nearby garrison walls, but he has no interest in my wanderings beyond my insolence and disobedience. It will be upon his own head should tragedy befall those poor people. You who find this diary will also find the secret I hold and the finder shall be privy to what only I know. I pray papa frees me before it is too late.

Genevieve Parker

"Wow!" we exclaimed in simultaneous whispers of awe. "1619! That paper is over 400 years old!" I deduced.

"Do you think Genevieve ever told her father what her secret was?" wondered Marley. "And what people is she talking about?"

"Well, I don't know but judging from the dates in the crypt, I'd guess that she didn't." I answered. "She died when she was fourteen years old."

"I had no idea! I wasn't paying attention to the dates, I guess." Marley replied. "Her mother died the year before, and her brother, Harold, died as an infant, so poor Genevieve must have been sad and lonely. It sounds like her father was some sort of trader, doesn't it?" I mused.

"She does refer to his "comings and goings" in her diary." agreed Marley.

"Well, in any case, neither of them is alive now, and all we have is this one page from her diary, so I guess her secret died with her." I said.

Marley concurred. "It does look that way. But the fact remains, we need to take a look around and figure out a way out of here. Maybe we'll come across the rest of her long, lost diary and find her secret while we're at it!"

"Now who's the dreamer?" I teased. "But you're right, we do need to come up with a plan, and we aren't going to do it sitting in this dank place. We'd better take a look outside. Maybe whoever lives here now can help us out."

Now, wandering around a nice, familiar cemetery in the dark is one thing, but venturing into the unknown is quite another, so neither of us was racing to open the door. In customary fashion, whenever the two of us were up against something big, we linked arms and slowly slid the door open together. The hinges groaned in protest, and something skittered across the floor.

"There goes your brother's gerbil!" I whispered.

For that comment I got another famous Marley punch and I vowed to keep my mouth shut lest I end up in a cast. On second thought, that would be one way to save myself from further humiliation at the ball park. But explaining how I ended up in the cast would be worse, so I clamped my lips shut and symbolically turned the key to my lips.

Outside the night air was brisk and filled with the sounds of chirping crickets and a lone owl, hooting forlornly. The full moon in a midnight sky spattered with billions of stars cast a blue glow, giving us a surprisingly clear view of the lay of the land. We could see what looked to be the main house about 100 yards in front of us, and a barn that had seen better days off to our left. Thinking our chances would be better at the house, we set off in the dewy grass, hoping someone inside could help us find our way home.

And maybe, just maybe, there'd be some nice, fresh, crisp-chewy chocolate chip cookies cooling on the counter.

As we gingerly stepped through the high, wet grass and approached the back of the house, we saw a dilapidated porch that looked none too sturdy. That, along with the fact that we saw no lights in that part of the house, had us rounding the corner, making our way to the front. I saw no garage, and no cars, and I didn't think anyone would park much in the old barn. I was not getting a good feeling, but I kept my thoughts to myself. My arm couldn't take much more pummeling, and I was nearly deaf as it was.

We made our way carefully around the front corner of the house and stopped dead in our tracks. The front porch, or what had been the front porch, no longer existed. The door was a good five feet above the ground and looked like it was floating in the absence of any steps leading up to it. We looked in the opposite direction, hoping for streetlights or some sign of life, any sign of life. Instead, we found ourselves staring at an endless driveway that disappeared between enormous evergreen trees. We turned back to the house, arms linked even tighter, and just stood there in silence. My heart felt like it had dropped to my knees by now, and Marley's face reflected her own hopelessness.

"Now what, Sir Jake?" she wailed. "It's pretty obvious that nobody has lived here in a verrrry long time and the road is a million miles away and we don't even know what road is out there!"

The pitch of Marley's voice rose with each word she uttered and my ears began tingling in anticipation of a full blown, shrieking assault. I knew I had to think fast, but, despite my vast stores of knowledge, I had no experience in dealing with such dire circumstances. I gave it my best shot as my fingers hovered alongside my head.

"Well, Mar," I said calmly, "you and I can pretty much handle anything, right?" I was hoping to boost her confidence, and maybe mine too. "So, I think our best chance is to find a way into the house, have a look around, and go from there. The worst that can happen is that we spend the night here and work our way home in the daylight."

I said all this in my supremely confident twelve year old, squeaky-deep voice. I would have crossed my fingers, but my ears were depending on them, so I just waited anxiously for her reply.

"You're right." she conceded quietly and I began to breathe normally again. "But I think we'd be better off trying our luck out back since neither of us can fly. Let's roll."

We reluctantly returned to the rear of the house, cautiously picking our way up the rickety back steps until we stood at the back door. We stopped and stared at the door for a minute, gathering our courage. Any paint that might have once dressed up the door had long peeled away so it was impossible to determine what color it might have been. There was a window in the upper part of the door, but it was so grimy with age that all we could see was a tattered piece of what might have been a curtain hanging inside. Together we reached for the rusty knob, gave each other a nod, and turned. The knob squealed in protest and wobbled as though it might fall out as we rotated it slowly to the right.

Marley gave a shocked gasp as the door creaked inward.

Chapter 4

After wiping the shroud of cobwebs from our faces, the first thing we noticed as we entered the house was the odor of OLD. It was that musty, dried up old paper smell that clogs up your nose and makes you sneeze like a maniac. This is exactly what we did until our eyes were watering and we could barely catch a breath between nasal explosions. Finally our noses settled down to occasional twitching and we took stock of what we could see.

We were standing in the kitchen but that was about all we knew for sure. Moonlight and candlelight aren't the best when you're trying to investigate, and we had left our night vision goggles at home. Slowly we walked around the table in front of us, a wooden rectangle large enough to seat eight with elbow room. There was a red and white checkered tablecloth, or what was left of one after various critters had nibbled on it, hanging in tatters from the heavy table. A large ceramic bowl sat in the center, home to three shriveled apple cores. Along one wall sat a giant wood burning stove, with four burners on its massive top, and two doors on the front of it. Upon one of the burners sat a black cast iron frying pan as though someone had been about to prepare a meal. As we rounded the end of the table we came upon a large wooden icebox. My grandma had one in her house, but she had used it as a table since refrigerators had been invented a while ago. We turned the brass latch on the door to explore inside and found the only contents were mouse droppings. The absence of modern appliances told us it had been a verrrry long time since anyone had eaten here. Needless to say, there were no crisp-chewy chocolate chip cookies cooling on the counter. In fact, I was pretty sure that, like electricity and indoor plumbing, they hadn't even been invented yet!

Next to the icebox was a door leading to a closet. I reached out and turned the knob tentatively, half expecting to come across a skeleton. Behind me Marley sucked in a breath, apparently sharing my grisly thought. We were relieved to find that, in addition to the usual straw broom and metal dust pan, all that hung there were an old yellow oilcloth coat and hat, under which a pair of well worn black rubber boots lay in tatters.

At the opposite end of the kitchen was a stairway leading to the upstairs, but we weren't quite ready to brave that unknown. We had pretty much figured out that the possibility of flipping a light switch was out of the question, and with only one candle between us, the idea of moving too deeply into the unknown bowels of the house did not appeal to either of us.

"Let's just see what the next room looks like." Marley suggested. "It will be even harder to see what's there without the moonlight but we can't spend the night in the kitchen. Maybe it will be like a living room with at least a sofa and a chair or two."

"Right behind you." I replied as we moved slowly through the doorway, perfectly willing to let her lead the way.

The next room did indeed look to be a living room from the shadows we could glimpse. The flickering candlelight did little to settle our nerves as we peered at the shapes of furniture around the room, when suddenly we heard a crashing sound overhead.

"AAAAAAAAAAAAAAAAAAHHHHHHHHHHHHH HHHH!" came the blood-curdling scream, right on cue.

Unfortunately I didn't have time to bring my fingers in contact with my ears, and now all I heard was the vibrating echo of her scream in the empty house. The news got even worse when we both realized that in her terror, Marley had dropped the candle, which now lay extinguished in a puddle of melted wax on the bare wood floor. The good news was we didn't set the place on fire in the process, but now we were really flying blind.

"I'm sorry Jake. I can't believe I'm such a *girl*." Marley said in a mixture of shame and disgust.

"It's okay, Mar. I would have done the same thing." I reassured her. "Except for the screaming thing." I added.

"Fair enough, Jake, but now what are we going to do without any light at all?" she worried. A tremor worked its way down her spine as her voice shook with the question.

"I'll go back into the kitchen. There must be matches somewhere if all they had was wood and candles around.

If we're lucky, they'll still be dry enough to catch. Wait here."

"You are right out of your mind if you think I'm waiting in here by myself, Jake Diggs! I'm with you." she exclaimed.

Once again we linked arms and made our way back into the kitchen, our need for light obliterating all thoughts of the reason for the sound above us for now. I rummaged along a shelf above the stove and said a silent prayer of thanks when my fingers curled around a small box. Eureka! A box of matches, and there were actually a few left in the box!

Of course, neither of us had thought to grab the candle off the floor, so we shuffled our arm-linked selves back into the living room in the dark. Marley picked up the candle and I struck the match along the strip on the side of the box. After three tries it lit and I had the candle going again.

"Maybe we can find other candles or maybe even a lantern if we look around." came Marley's brilliant suggestion.

"Way to go Mar!" I congratulated her, thankful for her logical thinking. "Let's see what we can come up with. It'll be pretty tough to find our way around with only the candlelight to go by."

My unspoken thought was of the sound that had caused the candle incident in the first place, but I'd keep it to myself for now. There was no point it lighting a fire under Marley's already shaky nerves.

Luckily there were no more crashes, shufflings, or bumps in the night as we worked our way through the sparsely furnished living room. Other than an old moth eaten sofa that might have been of a bright plaid once, there were two wooden high back chairs on either side of a small round table, coated with dust, all arranged around a ratty looking hooked rug in the center of the floor. On the table, miraculously, was an old oil lantern. Both the bottom well and the hurricane on top were glass, and we could see there was a small bit of oil left in the bottom. Critters had not been able to crawl inside the narrow opening at the top, so I was hopeful that the old cotton wick was still intact and the well wouldn't be too dry feed oil to the flame.

Marley lifted the hurricane off the base and I held the candle flame to the wick, deciding to reserve the matches for future lighting emergencies. The wick caught and held and we let out a small whoop of excitement as Marley replaced the hurricane top. Although there wasn't much oil, it gave us hope that we'd come upon other lanterns as we searched the rooms. Now that we had the lantern, we could move more quickly and avoid bumping into anything along the way.

"Looks like there's a doorway to the right." I pointed out. "Let's see what we can find in there.

"I think we ought to be looking for the rest of Genevieve's diary while we're at it.

Maybe we can find out what her secret was." said Marley.

"I haven't seen anything so far but that's another great idea. You're on a roll, Mar!" I responded, patting her on the back. "We'll keep our eyes peeled from now on."

Now that we had more light to work with we were feeling calmer and thoughts of the diary had returned. How that was possible since we had no idea where we were I can't say, but it's amazing how quickly the strange and unfamiliar can become almost normal. I do know it was definitely easier to continue our exploration without being linked at the arms. Now if I could just keep Marley from screaming again we might survive this crazy adventure.

The next room was small, too small to be of much use. As we came through the doorway we could see a closed door to our left, and a bench with a high back that had four hooks along the top along the wall. There was another table, a smaller version of the round one in the living room, to our right. On the opposite wall was a huge mirror in a heavily carved wooden frame, at least six feet tall. We turned toward the door, hesitantly trying to decide whether or not to open it. As I reached for the knob, Marley grabbed my arm.

"Wait, Jake. We don't know what's on the other side of that door." came her warning squeak.

"That's right, Mar, and we never will if we don't open it." I pointed out patiently, as if talking to a small child. "We'll do the link and you can close your eyes while I open it. If I don't pass out, that will be your signal to open your eyes, okay?"

"Don't be ridiculous." Marley huffed indignantly. "I don't need to close my eyes." she continued as her arm snaked through mine.

"Okay, on the count of three, I turn the knob. Ready?" I asked.

Marley nodded silently, gripping my arm a little tighter, as I began the countdown.

"One." The grip grew tighter. "Two." The eyes slammed shut.

"Three!" I exclaimed as I pulled the door open.

A few seconds went by before Marley responded. I was nice enough to stare straight ahead while she opened her eyes once she realized I was still standing there in her grip.

We stared through the open door, into the deep, dark night. We had discovered the front door, the one floating several feet above the ground. We shut the door again, turning around, and only then realized what we had missed on our first scan. There on the table sat another lantern. By now we were feeling pretty lucky and Mar actually did a little dancing spin move right there in the foyer as I picked up this latest treasure. I just rolled my eyes. Then I got punched…again.

Rubbing what now must be the biggest, deepest bruise ever recorded in medical history, I turned and strode back into the living room, carrying both lanterns. That, of course, left Marley in the dark, causing her to scurry into the living room where she promptly ran right into me. I gave her a pointed look and handed her the unlit lantern.

"If you're done bustin' a move maybe we can scope out the upstairs." was my scornful comment.

"You're just jealous, Diggs, because you don't have the moves." came Marley's haughty reply. With a flip of her blonde ponytail she started to walk across the room and back into the kitchen toward the stairs. Until she realized I was the one with the light, and I hadn't budged an inch. Well, to be fair, she did have the candle, but once you're used to lantern light, that's like trying to hit a homer with a toothpick. She waited, hand on her hip, until I got over myself and joined her trek across the living room floor.

"Truce?" I pleaded. "This is no time to get on each other's nerves."

"Truce!" Marley replied, and we shook hands on it as we stood at the bottom of the stairs that disappeared into darkness and more of the unknown.

It was then that we recalled the ominous crashing sound we had heard overhead earlier, and now neither of us was in a hurry to climb those stairs.

Attempting to appeal to Marley's logical side, I said. "It's been a while since we heard that noise and it's been quiet ever since. The wind probably blew something over, or maybe a field mouse ran into something or another."

"You're probably right." Marley bravely agreed. Link.

"Okay, pal, up we go." My own voice sounded braver than I felt as I put my right foot on the first step. "Let's take our time, in case any of the steps have rotted.

One by one, arm in arm, we took the steps, a total of eight, creaking under our combined weight until we reached a small landing where the stairs continued at a right angle to our left. "So far, so good", I thought. I held the lantern higher and counted; only five more to go. We began again, reaching the upstairs hall without crashing through a tread or breaking a leg. Sighs of relief escaped our lips until we realized we were facing three closed doors.

"Which one is the bathroom?" asked Marley, apparently needing to know this for a reason.

"Uh, Mar, I don't think any of them is a bathroom."

"Arrrgh, you're right! I can hold it." she said through clenched teeth.

"Okay, would you like Door #1, Door #2, or Door #3?" I asked, imitating an old TV game show host.

"Eeny, meeny, miney moe, catch a Goony by the toe. If he hollers, let him go; eeny, meeny miney moe!" chanted Marley as she pointed to a door with each word of the rhyme, ending up on the door to the left.

"Very clever!" I chuckled as we turned to open the door.

This time Marley reached down and turned, pushing the door open slowly. We walked into a small bedroom where faded curtains billowed at the broken window. Perhaps we had located the source of the sound that nearly rendered me deaf. We walked to the window and stopped when we heard and felt a crunching beneath our cleats.

Bingo! There on the floor were shards of glass, its former shape unknown to us now. "Well, at least now we know what the crashing sound was", I said, turning away from the table. I raised the lamp in front of me and we took in the rest of the meager furnishings.

An old iron bed with a plain white spread took up most of the room. Along one wall was a wooden dresser, on top of which sat a ceramic pitcher inside a large bowl. Both were painted with a blue flowery design. Above the dresser hung an oval mirror, and a silver hairbrush was the only other object on the dresser. There were no other doors, so it was easy enough to see there was no diary in this room. We searched the dresser drawers, just in case, but they were completely empty.

We exited that bedroom and moved to the next door down the hall. This room was larger, holding a double bed with a heavy wooden headboard that looked hand made. In addition to a similar dresser there was a tall bureau and a small table that sat next to one side of the bed. There was also another door in one wall, which is where we started our search. Hanging from hooks in the closet were two long, old-fashioned dresses, both with flowery prints, high collars, and lots of buttons. There was a man's suit, black and heavy, and two pairs of sturdy boots, one pair smaller than the other.

"This must be the parents' bedroom." I said. "Jonas and Johanna."

"Yeah, and it looks like they didn't have much, judging from the few outfits that are here." scoffed Marley.

"Different times pal." I said.

I reached in and peered past the clothing but saw nothing more in the closet. We decided then to start searching the drawers in case the diary might be hidden in one of them.

One by one we opened drawers, most of which were empty. A few contained underclothes; one drawer held a packet of letters tied up with a blue ribbon and another offered up a small notebook whose entries appeared to be in a man's handwriting.

Marley decided to hang on to these items. Having examined every available surface, space, and drawer, we concluded this room held no secrets waiting to be discovered. We'd look at the letters and notebook later, we decided, and shut the door behind us as we reentered the hall.

"One more to go, Mar," I said. "Last chance to reveal the secrets of Miss Genevieve Parker."

"It's got to be in there, Jake." Mar replied with a hint of desperation in her voice.

Feeling both desperate and hopeful, we turned the knob of the last bedroom and knew this was Genevieve's room. The single bed was neatly made with a pink floral spread.

This time the pitcher and bowl had pink roses adorning them. There was a dresser and mirror matching those in the first bedroom, and a small vanity table with a wooden stool beneath it. On the vanity were a hand mirror, brush, and comb, all of ornately engraved silver. A small blue bottle held a bit of liquid that still carried the faint scent of lilacs when Marley removed the glass stopper. In the small center drawer was a mother-of- pearl hair comb. Again there was a closet, its contents mirroring that of her parents bedroom, minus the suit and mans boots.

A search of the drawers revealed little more than under clothes and another packet of letters, this one tied with a pink ribbon. We turned to the small bedside table, and beside me Marley emitted a small, wondrous gasp of delight.

There it was, lying next to the lantern. Genevieve's diary, in her neatly lettered hand, lay closed upon the table. Marley picked up the brown leather-bound book and held it reverently, awestruck that it lay out in the open, so easily discovered. She hugged the small notebook to her, the look on her face knowing and certain.

"The secret is in here, Jake, I just know it!" she exclaimed. But before we could decide what to do next, the lantern in my hand sputtered out. At that same moment a faint scratching sound came from deep within the closet, followed by a soft moaning sound.

"AAAAAAAAAAAAAAAHHHHHHHHHHH HHHHHH!" tore the scream from Marley's throat as she fainted to the floor.

Chapter 5

With my ears ringing from Marley's latest assault on my now severely challenged eardrums, I reached into my pocket for the box of matches. There wasn't much I could do in the dark, so I slowly fumbled toward the bedside table, being careful to avoid tripping over my unconscious best friend. Cautiously I searched the top until my hand closed around the lantern we had seen there earlier. I didn't want to knock that over and eliminate what little chance I had of shedding light on what were quickly deteriorating into dire circumstances. I know; you're wondering why I didn't just go for our trusty candle. Well, what I failed to mention is that while we were investigating the first bedroom, the wind from the broken window had extinguished that source, and we decided the lantern we had was sufficient. The candle now lay discarded somewhere on the floor. Okay, sometimes twelve year olds don't know *everything*.

I struck a match, set it to the wick, and immediately a soft glow filled the room once again. I took an accounting of our precious matches before placing them back in my pocket, and realized we had only three more left. Judging from the amount of oil in this lamp, I figured we'd be okay for maybe an hour. Then I bent to check on my prone partner.

After first making sure Mar was still breathing I set the lantern out of her reach, because you never know what she's going to do, and began shaking her gently as I called her name. I let go a huge sigh of relief when, after just a few shakes, Marley began to come around. Slowly her eyes focused on my face and I knew my sidekick was back in action.

"Geez, Mar, you scared the snot right out of me!" I scolded. "The next time you feel one of your world-class screams coming on, could you warn me first? I think you might have a career in Hollywood ahead of you working on a horror movie set.

"Thanks for your concern, Jake." was Marley's sarcastic retort. "I could've had a heart attack or a concussion or broken bones, and all you care about are your stupid eardrums!"

"Be fair, Mar," I continued, a bit dramatically perhaps. "I revived you, didn't I, despite the fact that if we DO make it back home, I'll probably need to be fitted for double hearing aids."

"What do you mean IF we make it home?" she squeaked.

"Sorry Mar, it was a mere slip of the tongue. Of course I meant WHEN we make it home." I apologized. "Now, are we going to sit here and argue semantics or are we going to try to figure out exactly what is going on around here?"

I helped Marley return to her feet and we sat on Genevieve's bed, setting the lantern on the table. She set the diary, still unopened, on her lap. Now we had two mysteries to solve. Would the secret from the page we had found in the crypt be revealed in the pages of Genevieve's diary, and what was the scratching and moaning we had heard coming from the closet? Personally, I would have been happy to skip the closet mystery, scan the diary, and find our way back to cozy little Marble Manor. But, no, Marley the Brave just had to know it all. Girls could be such a pain sometimes.

"Let's check out the closet first, Jake. I want to make sure nobody is trapped in there." Marley proposed.

"Mar, nobody has even lived here since the Dark Ages. How could anyone survive if they were trapped in the closet?" I reasoned, rolling my eyes toward heaven.

"Well something made that noise Mr. Know-It-All, and I want to know what that something was!" Marley replied in a huff.

"Fine, we'll check it out. But first I need to find that candle again. If this lantern goes out we're done for, and we left the other lantern in the foyer downstairs."

I grasped the lantern and the two of us stood. We quickly scanned the floor and found the candle near the dresser, then we strode to the closet door in five steps, much too quickly for my liking. I reached for the knob on the closet door, holding the lantern as far out in front of me as I could, and began to turn.

I nearly jumped out of my skin when Marley shouted, "Wait!"

Oh yeah, how could I forget? She linked her arm around mine, then turned to face the door. This whole experience was getting to me. Again, my hand assumed its position on the doorknob, and slowly I brought the door open. The same two dresses still hung there, but the rest of the closet looked like a black hole. The good news is there wasn't a pair of glowing yellow eyes staring back at us. But on the other hand, who knew what *was* lurking in the shadowy depths. A felt a shudder rumble through my body, and then came the punch. I wasn't sure how much more of Marley's pummeling I could take as I whipped my head around to glare at her.

"Don't even look at me that way Diggs!" said Marley indignantly, as if she actually had a good reason for growing my bruise. "How am I supposed to hang tough with you standing there shaking like a leaf?"

"My sincerest apologies, your highness," I replied, bowing low. "I shall control my involuntary nervous reactions from now on and keep my deepest fears to myself!"

"I would appreciate that." she replied demurely. "After all, you are the fearless dragon slayer and I am but a fair maiden."

Between my rolling eyes, ringing ears, and throbbing arm, all I wanted to do was plop down on my nice soft couch at home and gorge on soft, flat chocolate chip cookies, even if it did mean rehashing the game with my pop. Even the game seemed like a distant memory now, absent of the humiliation and dread that had dogged me before our world turned upside down in the crypt. Suddenly I almost felt like hugging Goony Graves!

This was absolutely the longest night of my life and I was ready for it to be over.

I swallowed any further retorts and slid slowly into the closet. The space was barely wide enough for us to stand side by side, but it was probably twice as deep as that. We noticed a shelf above us where a couple of round boxes reposed. Marley was kind enough to enlighten me with an explanation that these were hat boxes, a fact I could have remained happily ignorant of. She reached up and brought them down and we discovered they held…hats. No surprises there, but then I considered that to be a good thing just about now.

We took another step and the back wall was inches from our faces. In the confined space, the lantern illuminated just about every visible surface, so we were able to clearly see the walls and floor. Marley dropped to her knees and began gently tapping, first along the floor, and then along the three lower walls.

"What's with the tapping, Super Sleuth?" I kidded.

"For your information, genius, I am listening for hollow spots that might be a trap door." Marley relied superiorly.

It sounded like a good plan to me, but I wasn't in the mood to share that with her, so I kept my praise to myself. The tapping continued for another minute and then stopped as suddenly as it had begun. I wasn't sure whether I should be thrilled or terrified, but I didn't have to wonder for long.

"Jake!" whispered Marley in a voice that sounded both excited and fearful at the same time. "Did you hear that?

"Mar, I can barely hear anything after all of your screaming." I said, covering my arm at the same time.

"No, seriously," she continued, ignoring my snide remark. "That last tapping sound? I didn't do that! It came from the *other* side of the wall!"

Well, at least now I knew how I should be feeling… terrified! There couldn't possibly be a sane and reasonable explanation for the responding taps, and I knew Marley wouldn't rest until she had one. Before I knew it, she was busy working her fingers into a small knothole in a board where she heard the tapping. Off it came and she laid it on the floor before moving on to a neighboring board. In minutes there were seven boards piled on the floor, and a hole in the wall big enough for her to crawl through. I say her because she's about four inches shorter and 25 pounds lighter, which meant she had my vote for "Most Likely to Crawl Through the Wall". I would nobly stand guard here in the closet, ready to grab her foot and yank her back out if she ran into trouble, but secretly I was thrilled because at least now if she screamed, I would be far enough away to avoid being plunged into total and irreversible deafness.

Of course that brilliant idea evaporated the second Marley took the lantern from me and said. "Let's roll, Jake."

"L-l-let's r-r-roll?" I stammered, convinced my waning hearing capabilities had played a trick on me. "Y-y-you mean as in 'us'? You *and* me?" I weakly queried, eyeing the whole in the wall dubiously.

"Well, you don't think I'm going in there all by myself, do you? Are you completely out of your mind?" Marley whined, the edge in her voice apparent as with each syllable she came closer and closer to shriek status.

"Mar, be fair!" I cried. "You can barely fit through that hole. How am I supposed to squeeze myself in there and expect to come out in one piece?

Now it was Marley's turn to roll her eyes, but I refrained from punching her in the arm. Somehow the rules on who could hit who were slightly different, although I wasn't sure why. Fair is fair, I thought, but some survival gene leftover from cave man days kicked into gear and advised that I'd be safer keeping my hands to myself.

"Jaaake," Marley said slowly, as though I had suddenly morphed into a three year old. She continued to speak slowly and deliberately as she explained, "I will remove a few more boards so that you can fit through the hole. But I think the problem has more to do with the size of your head than your height." she ended smartly.

"Very funny," I replied snidely. "Go ahead, Marvelous Marley the Magnificent, pry off a few more boards and we'll go see if we can find ourselves a ghost."

Then I stood there stubbornly, arms folded across my chest, as Marley groaned and returned to her task. After prying away three more boards, which meant nearly one entire side of the closet wall had been demolished by now, she stood, brushing her hands on the thighs of her uniform. She stooped to pick up the lantern.

"Lead the way, Sir Jake of Diggs, Dragonslayer and World Class Chicken!" was Marley's comment as she handed the lantern to me with a flourish of arm and a low bow.

I had had just about enough of her bossiness and superiority by now, and my next move helped me regain some of my precious manly ground. Without warning I turned and walked out of the closet, through the door not the wall, and returned to the bedroom. This, of course, left Marley standing in the dark closet…alone. I couldn't help but think I had gotten sweet revenge, but my smugness was soon put in check when I heard the warning yelp coming from the closet. I heard a shuffling and scrambling coming from the closet and held the lantern in that direction. Out spilled Marley, landing on all fours as she tripped her way back into the bedroom.

"Ooooohhhh, you are such a jerk, Jake Diggs." she fumed. She tried to stand but got tangled up in her own limbs and landed with a soft thud on her butt.

"Sorry, Mar." I said innocently. "I just remembered that we might need the candle again in case the lantern goes out, so I came back to get it." Even as I said the words with a smile, I secretly congratulated myself for my cleverness. That ought to put her in her place!

"Good idea." came Marley's reluctant reply. "Now can we please get this over with before I lose my nerve?"

"Aha! A chink in the armor." was the thought that placed me back in my own good graces. Once again the caveman gene took over and I decided not to rub it in as I walked over to help Marley back to her feet. Besides, her response kind of took the wind out of my sails, deflating my ego and my attitude. We had no idea what time it was, not the hour, the day, or for that matter, even the year anymore. I knew I was feeling dog- dead tired, but there was too much of the unknown out there for either of us to consider taking a rest. Before we left the room, Marley grabbed the diary and the packets of letters.

"Here, put this in the back of your pants. Who knows if we'll end up back here, and I think we're better off taking these with us. It's not like anybody's going to come looking for them." said Marley as she tucked the letters in to the back waistband of her pants and handed me the diary. "You never know; if this situation gets any worse, maybe something written in these could help us."

"You've got it, pal." I replied as I stuffed the diary into my own pants. "I hope we find something that helps us out of this predicament soon because right now I feel like I could down at least five dozen crisp-chewy chocolate chip cookies and a gallon of ice cold milk, then sleep for two months."

"Dittoe, pal. I'm so tired I don't think I'd know the difference between a ghost and my own mother." sighed Marley heavily.

We gave each other a sympathetic, we're-in-this-together look, then crossed back over to the closet. I handed Marley the candle that had been in my back pocket, then got down on my knees. I lit her candle before placing the lantern on the other side of the hole, then crawled through to the other side. I held the lantern up to the opening so Marley could find her way, then we both got to our feet and she blew out the candle. Brushing filmy cobwebs from our faces for the second time tonight, we looked ahead and hesitantly began our journey into the unfathomable darkness that lay before us.

Chapter 6

We could see nothing but unending pitch–dark beyond the small pool of light cast by the lantern. There was a faint smell of cold, wet dirt but no other clues to tell us where we might end up. In a space barely wide enough for us to stand side by side, we linked and slowly started walking into the sinister space. We kept our eyes trained on the floor, lest we should come across any obstacles, living or dead that might trip us up. The walls and ceiling seemed to be made of the same kind of boards Marley had torn away from the closet wall. The floor felt and smelled like hard packed damp earth and reminded me of the lake road where we had a cottage back in the real world.

Neither of us said a word as we picked our way along for a distance of maybe eight feet. Suddenly we found ourselves moving down an incline, some kind of ramp I guess, but definitely heading down. Our descent continued for perhaps ten or twelve more feet before leveling off and angling to the right. The odor of damp earth was stronger now, and the air felt about ten degrees cooler. I felt Mar give a shudder next to me, but explained it away with the unexpected drop in temperature. After just a few steps the tunnel angled left and we again felt the path slope further downward. So far the path had been surprisingly free of anything that might have crawled in and died, a fact we were both grateful for. The walls and ceiling were all of dirt now, with an occasional thick beam spanning the ceiling for support. Finally the ground seemed to level off again, but the depth of the darkness hadn't let up at all so we had no idea how much further we might have to go.

We stopped for a minute, checking the lantern to see how our oil supply was holding up.

"I hope we don't have much farther to go," I worried. "I'd say we have maybe fifteen minutes of light left here before we have to resort to the candle."

"I feel a slight breeze now, which means the candle might not even stay lit." returned Marley. "I wish we had grabbed that lantern in the foyer, but maybe the breeze is a sign that we're close to finding a way out." she said hopefully.

Having made it this far without encountering any scuttering, skittering, or slithering creatures, we focused our eyes on our surroundings, trusting the path would remain clear. I guessed that we were probably underground now judging from the cold, damp air and musty earth smell. The ceiling overhead seemed somewhat closer, but the path was widening now. Both the walls and ceiling seemed made of hard-packed earth in this section, with wide timbers every three or four feet to add strength. On the wall timbers were hooks which might have held candles or lanterns at one time. I'd have gladly lit them but they had apparently been removed long ago. Then the darkness ahead shifted slightly and we came upon our next dilemma

"Now what?" asked Marley, bewildered by what we had discovered. "Good question." I replied, as baffled as she was.

We faced not one, but two tunnels, split like a Y from where we stood. Neither looked promising, and now we had to calculate our next move.

"Are you wearing a watch?" I asked, an idea taking shape in my mind.

"Yes, but why is that important?" Marley asked with a hint of impatience tingeing her reply.

"Well, I have an idea," I ventured slowly, anticipating that she wouldn't like my idea one little bit. "So far we haven't run into anyone or anything really scary or dangerous, right?"

"Riiight," she cautiously agreed.

"Well, I was thinking that since we have a lantern and a candle, maybe we could split up and meet back here in, say, five minutes. Five minutes isn't long and before you know it we'll be back here comparing notes." I said encouragingly, sounding more courageous than I actually felt.

Marley didn't respond but I could tell she was weighing the options, most likely looking for reasons why it shouldn't, couldn't, wouldn't work. Hopefully she wouldn't be so disgusted that she'd punch me again. It had been a while and I was almost hopeful I'd make a full recovery.

"Come on, Mar, what do you think?" I gently prodded. "We don't have much time left on this lantern oil.

My trusty friend and hotshot shortstop finally gave me her answer. "I get the lantern." she insisted.

I grinned like a jack O' lantern on Halloween and handed it over to her. She lifted the hurricane and I lit the candle from the lantern wick, holding my hand to keep the meager flame from blowing out. We clicked candle to lantern in a little "cheers" move to wish each other luck, synchronized our watches, and then stood back to back, each facing a different tunnel. We spent a minute discussing strategy, like what to look and listen for, before checking our watches once again. The bad news then was that it was 11:55 PM, which only served to remind us that we should have been home in Marble Manor, dreaming of the next big win. I wondered if our parents had sent out search parties or called the police yet, and thought that they must be as frightened as we were. My mother's crying face swam before me, motivating me to get on with this so we could find our way back home. On the count of three we each trekked off down our tunnels and began our separate missions, having agreed to meet back in this very spot in precisely five minutes.

I made my way down the tunnel to the left having watched for a moment as Marley disappeared to the right. I said a silent prayer that we'd both make it back in one piece, and tried to pick up my pace, hoping to return first so Marley wouldn't have to wait and wonder alone. Sir Jake, the Dragon Slayer was back. Okay, maybe not, but I was trying.

I walked for the first two minutes and this branch of the tunnel seemed no different than the main tunnel had been. I knew that I'd have to turn back soon, with nothing to report. Maybe Marley had had better luck, I thought, before deciding to go just a few more steps before I turned around. I'd make better time on the return trip anyway, being familiar with the way now, I reasoned, so I took another ten steps forward before I stopped dead in my tracks. The light from the candle was far too dim to be revealing, but the eerie silence meant that I couldn't miss the unmistakable sound of footsteps shuffling overhead. I actually placed the candle carefully on the earth next to me, hoping that I'd be able to see if there was also a light from above. My twelve-year-old brilliance was rewarded as I spied light seeping through cracks in the wood in the ceiling. It looked to be a sort of trap door, as it had hinges and was the only part of the ceiling that wasn't earth or timbers. There was a large iron loop hanging from the side opposite the hinges. I reached for the loop before realizing I had no time to delve into this latest mystery.

Marley would be waiting and I didn't want her shrieking to give our position away.

I high-tailed it back to our meeting spot, panting but relieved that I had beat Marley back. I bent in half to catch my breath while I waited. All the while I wondered who and what we'd find if we opened that trap door, and if Marley had made a similar find.

Somewhere in my musing I realized that more than five minutes had passed and Marley hadn't turned up yet. I checked my watch and found more than ten minutes had passed, as I felt icy fingers of panic running up my spine and the back of my neck. She should have been back by now and the reason for her absence couldn't possibly be good. I had only one option and that was to set off down the right tunnel and find her. At least I knew what was down my tunnel, sort of. Now I had to dive into the unknown again and believe I'd find Marley sooner rather than later. I knew that when I did, I'd be begging her to punch me.

I hustled forward, trusting no obstacles awaited my flying feet, hurtling myself as fast as my candle would allow, down the dark passage. I came up short when I narrowly missed running headlong into a wall. I had found the end of the tunnel. What I hadn't found was Marley.

Chapter 7

My first instinct was to look up, and I wasn't disappointed. Above my head was another trap door, identical to the one I had found in my branch of the tunnel. Slivers of light seeped through the cracks in the boards. Along with them sifted the sound of muffled voices. I strained to make out their words, but all I could understand was that they were angry. The sudden scraping of chairs struck like a thunder clap in my silent cavern, making it difficult to hear anything other than the chattering of my teeth and the hammering of my heart.

I quickly began searching for some way to reach the door, something to climb up or on; anything that would bring me closer to Marley. It was then that I noticed the two packets of letters lying on the cold, damp floor. I was sure now that Marley was somewhere above me, but what I couldn't know was whether the letters had fallen when she had apparently been hauled out of the tunnel, or if she had left them as a clue to help me find her. I decided to go with the latter, bent to scoop up the letters, and stuck them into my now overcrowded waistband. Good thing I hadn't eaten in hours or there'd be no room for me with all this paper I was hauling around in my pants.

I came up empty, however, in my search for a means of climbing up to the door, and, judging from the angry tones I had heard, I decided my chances might be better back in my tunnel, where at least the sounds I had heard hadn't been angry men's voices. I could be back there in a matter of minutes, I reasoned, and if I could find a way up through that door, then I might stand a better chance of finding Marley above ground.

I tore back through the tunnels as fast as my flickering candle would allow, stopping only when I had reached what I hoped would be my portal to whatever world lay above me. After catching my breath, I stood listening, as I had moments before, for any signs of life above. Finally, from above my head, came music to my ears, literally. My prayers had been answered in the form of soft feminine humming floating over me on the dust moats slipping through the cracks in the trap door. The only thing that would have sounded better to me at that moment would be Marley's piercing shrieks. When I heard no other voices, I became determined to find a way out of this hole, certain that Marley couldn't be far away.

My search for a way up, short of sprouting wings and flying, which seemed entirely possible in this fantasy, came up empty. My frustration, fueled by an increasing sense of urgency, threatened to tear from my throat in a howl of rage, but I clamped my mouth shut to keep it from escaping. There wasn't so much as a stone I could throw against the wooden planks to alert whoever was up there of my existence. I had no other choice but to call out to whoever was humming and hope she'd lift the door, exposing me as either an intruder in her cellar or a poor, trapped boy who looked like he needed a good meal.

"HEY!" I began shouting. "Can anyone up there hear me?" "Help!" I added, working on the poor, hungry boy concept.

I stopped to judge the success of my shouts, and sure enough, the humming had ceased. Soft footfalls approached, stopping directly overhead. I crossed my fingers and willed the door to open. Silence…not a good omen. Perhaps I had frightened the girl and I'd have to take my chances with the angry men in the other passageway. Maybe if I called out once more and really tried to sound helpless, which I'm not, being twelve and all, she'd take pity on me and pull the door wide.

"Pleeease, help me" I said, with just a smidge of whining. "Is anyone there?" I pleaded, pouring on the "poor boy" act. Again, I waited.

Creeeeaaaak. Slowly the door opened and the breath I'd been holding spilled out in a relieved whooooosh. Suddenly I seemed to be standing in a spotlight, a welcome sight for sure. I could see a girl, about my own age, peering down at me, her face a mixture of caution and curiosity. Maybe I was starting to hallucinate, but she reminded me of my own sister, whom I suddenly missed. Now I was sure I was hallucinating!

I took in the small oval face and halo of dark curls as she lowered a ladder into my pit, apparently having decided I posed no threat to her. I blew out my pitiful candle and slowly ascended, rung by rung, until I stood on solid ground once again. I completed a 360 degree turn in slow motion, my brain registering nothing but shock. I even blinked a few times, trying to clear my vision as my eyes swept the space, but the images remained the same. I was back in the shed! The very same shed Marley and I had landed in after we were torn from our nice cozy crypt by whatever cosmic forces were at work here.

And there stood the humming girl, staring at *me*, as if I were some kind of alien. But to be fair, it probably wasn't every day she rescued baseball players from her cellar.

Now it was my turn to study her, and it was then I understood why she looked at me so strangely. She was dressed in a long, heavy-looking black dress that skimmed both her chin and the floor. Over that she wore an apron, and on her feet were sturdy black boots that, judging from the buttons that ran up the sides, ended somewhere above her ankles. Her dark, wavy hair was pulled back and ended in the middle of her back, framing a pale face that held the bluest eyes I'd ever seen. She was taller than Marley, and more slender and I'd bet she had never played shortstop in her life. Finally I broke the silence that was becoming awkward.

"Hi." I said, extending my hand, "I'm Jake."

"Greetings to you, Master Jake. My given name is Genevieve Parker, but you may call me Genny. I am pleased to meet you." she replied, speaking a type of English I had only read about in history books. She extended her hand and the introduction was completed with a quick shake.

"Um, uh, nice to meet you too, Genny." I stammered. "By any chance have you seen a girl dressed like me around here?"

Genny looked at me like I had antlers and a horn in the middle of my forehead. I took that as a no.

"A girl? In such an outfit as that?" she asked, alarm rising in her voice as she pointed at my uniform.

"Well, uh, yes. She plays on my baseball team, so she's wearing a uniform just like mine." I explained.

"Base ball? I know nothing of base ball." she exclaimed, splitting the name of my beloved sport into two separate words.

"It's a game. Don't the boys around here play?" I asked, bewildered yet at the same time knowing more than poor Genny did, since I was the one who had traveled through time.

"It doesn't matter," I reassured her. "What I really want to know is have you seen a girl anywhere near here? My best friend Marley is missing and I'm hoping to find her here."

"Thou hast lost a friend who is a girl and her given name is Marley?" she stammered, completely lost.

"Genny, let me explain what is happening. You may find it hard to believe, but the fact that I'm standing here in your shed talking to you should make my story pretty convincing."

She showed me to a chair near a table, and we sat as I brought her into my world while remaining solidly planted in hers. I started with what had happened in the cemetery, not wanting to go into a long lesson on base ball, and took her through the crazy tale, step by step. I told her how we had slipped into her family crypt to dodge a sudden rainstorm. What I didn't tell her was that we had seen her name inside because I didn't want another girl passing out on me. Judging from the dates I had read on her tomb, she didn't have much longer to live, a realization that now sent chills down my spine. I went on to explain that we had found the crumpled diary page, picked it up, and the next thing we knew we had landed in this very shed.

At first Genny listened intently, hanging on my every word. Every so often she gasped or exclaimed, but she held her curiosity until finally she burst forth with a question.

"If I may ask, what is the year of thy birth?" was her first inquiry. "I was born in 1993 and I just turned twelve last month."

Chapter 8

For the second time that night I found myself having to revive a girl who had passed out onto the floor. Maybe I would consider a career in medicine if I ever made it back to the real world in one piece. Luckily Genny had been sitting down so she didn't have far to go before she hit the floor. As I had earlier with Marley, I knelt down and began to gently shake Genny as I called her name. She let out a soft moan and then opened her eyes and for a moment I thought I was going to lose her again, but she rallied and tried to sit up. I helped her back to her chair, before looking around to see if I could get her a glass of water or something. I spotted a pitcher and poured her a mug of water, setting it on the table in front of her. She took a few sips then looked at me with eyes as clear as a summer sky. Now it was my turn to ask a question.

"Genny, when were *you* born?" I asked, not at all certain I wanted to hear her answer. At least I was pretty sure I wouldn't pass out when she told me.

"I was born in England on 24 August, 1605, and I will be fourteen next birthday.

I arrived here with my family one year past."

I was stunned. 1605? That meant that Genny was nearly 400 years older than me!

Now I understood why she had fainted because I was feeling a little woozy myself. Marley and I had been hurtled backward 400 years through time, and we had the advantage of knowing, at least roughly, the events and things that had occurred in that time. Genny, however, had no insight whatsoever into all the changes that had taken place since 1619. No wonder she was shocked that a girl would be dressed like me and had no idea what baseball was. Now all I had to do was figure out WHY we ended up here, how to find Marley, and then find a way back to the present time, and all before anyone home realized we had gone missing, assuming they hadn't already. No problem.

But for now I had to finish explaining to Genny what had happened so that she would be able to help me find Marley. She knew about the tunnels obviously, so she would know where the other branch led and how we could get to there from here, where I was certain Marley must be. Of course, Genny first had to believe my story, but I figured she was already on her way there since she seemed willing to talk to me and hadn't run away screaming in terror. But the minutes were ticking by and I had to give her the short version. I had no idea how much longer Marley would be safe; she might already be in terrible danger. There was no way I could show up back in Marble Manor alone, nor would I want to.

I proceeded to recount to Genny how Marley and I had left the shed and explored the house, our discovery of the closet, and finally our search of the tunnels. I slumped in my chair then, exhaustion threatening to overwhelm me as I sat for the first time all night, and waited. Genny's face had shown a mixture of surprise, disbelief, curiosity, and fear as I wound my way through the incredible chain of events that led me to be sitting here with her now.

"Thou say thy friend Marley has vanished from yon tunnel. I know not for certain but the barn is where she must be as the tunnel you speak of leads there. I dare not say who might hold her, nor if she is in danger, but I have my own story to tell before we can commence a search." Genny replied in her odd manner of speech. But, she did say she was born in England and it was the 17th century, so I guess that would explain it. I just hoped I could follow her story and that it would lead us to my friend. She began to weave her own amazing tale, parts of which I had studied in school, and I was mesmerized.

"I have said I hail from England and have come to Jamestown one year hence. I, mama, and papa sailed on a long journey, with five score or more, to be free in this new place. My brother passed in his infancy whilst we dwelt in the garrison, and mama remained sad these many years. The sailing trip was wretched and mama lived only three months after arriving here, one month after my brother's passing. Papa and I lived in the garrison with the others until this property was offered. He had known great wealth in England and remained in possession of such, though I know not by what means. He traded with the natives, muskets and gun powder, for this land. Papa is a traitor to arm the natives so, as they will turn the guns on us one day, but he dismissed me when I accused him of this. When my people treat them so poorly it is justice, neigh, revenge they will seek to retain what is rightfully theirs. Papa may think girls are useful only to care for the home and family, but I had lessons in England, which I proved good at. I work on my lessons here, and sometimes teach the younger ones in the garrison."

Genny continued her story, relating how difficult life was in her new home, with Indian raids and return fire from the garrison. Her papa seemed a busy man who shared little time with her, which left Genny on her own much of the time. I thought he must be crazy leaving a defenseless girl on her own outside the safety of the garrison.

"I have taken to walks in the woods when papa is long absent, meeting my friends, both English and native, where we play at games and teach each other our language. We swim in the river in summer, but winter is harsh and our meetings are few then. On one such recent walk, papa returned home sooner than expected and found me gone. It was when I returned that he locked me in this shed, a fortnight ago, and I have seen him not at all since then. But I have heard men's voices from the barn and in the tunnels, urgent and rushed, and I fear much misery shall be wrought through their deeds. As for when my imprisonment will end, my hope is fading."

Genny finished her story but left me with more questions than I had time to ask. I tried to think of those that would be most likely to lead me to Marley while encountering the least amount of danger.

"Have you heard what the men are saying?"

"I have on occasion heard talk of guns and gunpowder, and late of night I hear the wheeling of carts, heavily laden and slow moving, leaving the barn." came her reply.

Then she added, "When last I journeyed into the woods, my native friends spoke of many pow-wows amongst the chiefs with talk of war against the white man. I fear papa is part of what will be a terrible war. Jamestown can little afford to lose more men after so many years of harsh conditions and many deaths from so much hardship. If only the men could make peace as we children have." she finished wearily.

"Will the men be moving through the tunnel tonight?" I asked her. "Aye, every night these four nights past they have." she nodded.

"I have to get to the barn and see if Marley is in there before they start making their move. If they decide to make her part of one of their shipments, well, I can't even think about that. Will you help me?" I pleaded.

"Aye, Master Jake, I shall. There be a way in through the back they know nothing of, and we shall slip in there. You may then climb to the loft and peer downward; take care they do not see you. But, first we must find a way out of here. The tunnel is not safe; the men will be traveling to be sure the way is clear. Surprised I am that you were not discovered down there already, as papa always has a guard nearby to keep me from escaping. Perhaps they found your friend Marley."

"Let's roll," I said, rising from my chair. I doubted Genny had heard that phrase before, but she took my cue and rose from her chair. "There has to be another way out,"

I boldly claimed as I began to search the walls, thinking Marley's closet strategy might work here somehow. I tried the window first, knowing it was too obvious, only to discover I was absolutely right as it had been nailed shut. There had to be another way.

Chapter 9

Remembering that the barn was next to the shed but some distance away, I headed toward the back wall. My superior teenage brain had reasoned that we'd be better off trying to stay out of sight, so there was no need to start in the front. As Marley had done in the closet, I began tapping along the lower walls. Luckily there were no moans or responding taps from the other side. As I neared the corner where the back wall met the side I could feel the beginnings of panic rising in my rapid heartbeat and short, raggedy breaths. Not one board was loose, nor was there a single place to slip prying fingers into. I turned to the side wall as my breathing began to sound like machine gun fire in my ears. I very nearly let out a wild whoop of joy when, on the fourth board, I found just enough space to work my fingers behind the edge. I braced myself and begin to exert pressure, pulling the board toward me. I landed squarely on my butt, but I was grinning like a ghoul because there, in my hands, was the board.

I quickly applied my technique to the next few boards until I had created a space big enough for us to crawl through, even managing not to embarrass myself by toppling over again.

"Take care, Master Jake." warned Genny. The men will be about and there may be natives in yon woods, waiting to ambush papa and steal the weapons. We'll take no light with us, and we must crawl low to the ground."

I nodded in agreement and crawled slowly through the hole in the wall. Genny followed slowly, untangling her long skirts from around her legs as she stood. We crept around the back of the shed in silence until we had reached the corner and could see the barn across the yard. We stopped then to listen for any sounds that might tell us where danger lie ahead but only the night sounds met us. The moon was now hidden behind massive gray clouds in the inky sky, further helping us to avoid detection as we closed the space between the shed and the barn.

Arriving behind the barn we sat with our backs to the wall, ears alert once again for telltale signs of human company. Crickets sang and an owl hooted; a lone coyote howled in the distance, but no voices or crackling brush sounds returned.

"There is a place along this wall where we can loosen some boards and crawl inside." informed Genny. "Once inside, there will be a stairway to the loft where we may hide and listen to papa and his men. Perhaps then we will see your friend, or learn of her whereabouts. My friends and I sometimes use the loft so I know papa has nothing there and will have no need of it. We will be safe there."

Genny showed me the spot where I once again honed my demolition skills and we were inside in moments. The soft nicking of the horses was the only sound we heard and they didn't seem to mind our intrusion. We stealthily climbed the stairs, praying none of the treads would creak and give us away. So far there didn't seem to be any men about, but one can never be too safe. We emerged in the loft which had been loaded with hay, and made our way to the edge overlooking the space below. I could feel my nose twitch threateningly and quickly pinched it between my finger and thumb to hold back the sneeze lurking there. I managed to stifle the sneeze, but now I knew Marley wasn't in here because her hay fever would have given her away in a second, with rapid-fire nostril action that would have the horses rearing up in their stalls.

We chose the darkest corner and lay down to wait. We didn't dare speak. In our silence I reflected on the fact that Genny was neither a puncher, nor a screamer, for which I was undyingly grateful. I returned my focus to finding a way out of this pickle, but came up empty. I was beginning to think Marley and I were doomed to live out the rest of our days wearing baseball uniforms and never, ever tasting a crisp-chewy chocolate chip cookie again. I would have cried at that last thought if I weren't such an almightily superior twelve year-old boy. I wished right then and there that I was seven.

My pity-party came to an abrupt halt when the barn door swung open and a group of men, each carrying a lantern, trouped in. Genny and I both gasped slightly, then held that breath for fear the men had heard us. One stood guard near the open door, while three others moved to some crates lined up against the wall. One of them had a tool and began prying the lid off the first crate. Quickly they unloaded the contents, placing what looked to be several long guns in a wagon. Then came an equal number of long, slender rods, used for tamping the gunpowder in the musket barrels, followed by too many pouches to count, all containing the lethal balls that would be fired at whatever enemy dared to attack.

Turning to one of his partners, the tallest man spoke gruffly. "Cyrus, bring the interloper. The crate is empty and ready."

Cyrus left the barn and returned almost immediately with the crate's next load. How I kept myself from leaping onto Cyrus' back from my perch in the loft I'll never know, because the intended contents just happened to be my friend Marley! She had been tied at the wrists and a gag placed over her mouth, but she squirmed like a worm on a fish hook against her jailer.

I felt Genny's hand clutch my arm and I turned to her. She read the panic and rage on my face and placed one finger in front of her lips, signaling me to keep quiet. Her brilliant blue eyes silently urged me to stay calm and be patient. That was the last thing I wanted to do, but I knew we'd all be in greater danger if I played Superman now, so I nodded and tried to crush the impulse to save the day.

I watched miserably as Cyrus placed Marley in the crate, which looked too much like a coffin now, and then nailed the lid back on. He ordered his partners to load the crate into the wagon with the guns, and moved toward the back of the barn, directly beneath our loft. A door creaked below us and then came the sounds of a horse's hooves as Cyrus led a midnight black stallion into the barn and hitched him to the wagon. This horse was chosen for stealth and speed, I thought, feeling more doomed than ever. Once the men led that horse from the barn, how would I ever catch up to them and rescue Marley?

Despair descended like a great storm cloud upon me and I sagged in defeat.

Genny reached out to me again and, with a knowing look in her eyes, silently pleaded with me to trust her. I had no choice; she was my only link between the present and the past, and right now I wasn't sure which was which.

Cyrus and one of the men climbed up on the buckboard while the other two held both doors open. Out went the horse, the wagon, and Marley, into the deep, dark night. The doors closed and Genny and I were alone in the loft again as the remaining men followed.

"Master Jake," she whispered, "fear not, for I know where they shall go. Pray the natives do not find them first and we will be certain of saving your friend. You must trust me, Master Jake, and use care where we will go."

"I trust you," I said, "but could we please hurry. I promise not to do anything stupid but the sooner we leave, the easier it will be for me to keep that vow."

"Follow me and heed my words. We will be waiting for Marley before they arrive at their meeting place." Genny instructed, even as she began her descent from the loft.

I was right behind her when we entered the stalls again. Genny breezed into one of them and, after saddling one of the horses, led it to an upended crate in the main barn. I opened the barn door cautiously, just in case a guard was posted, then returned. Genny signaled for me to mount the horse. I had never been on anything more than a silly painted carousel horse in my brief life, and the cold sweat of fear began to run down my back. The chestnut mare seemed gentle enough, but I had a healthy respect for anything that could crush me to death, including Goony Graves. Being the gentleman I am, I indicated that she should go first, figuring she'd be better at controlling the beast, and then I climbed aboard. We left the barn and I closed my eyes.

Genny led the horse to the woods at a nice, slow pace, and I was beginning to feel like I might survive this latest adventure. I was breathing normally again until suddenly, the horse took off in full gallop, instinct leading it along an unseen path deep in the woods.

My eyes slammed shut again and now I didn't care if Genny thought I was a coward. I wrapped my arms around her and held on for dear life. After forever, or maybe ten minutes, the horse slowed again, its great heaving breaths shooting plumes of steam into the cool night air, and I relaxed my grip. Easing my eyes open, I took in our new surroundings. Thankfully, Genny never mentioned my suffocating death grip during the ride.

We had come to the edge of what must have been an native village, for there were no high stockade fences, nor towers with sharpshooters. Instead there were several longhouses, built to form a semi-circle. A great fire blazed in a large open area where several people were gathered, the smell of roasting meat filling my nostrils with yearning. My stomach growled and rumbled like thunder as my mouth watered at the delicious aroma. Until now I had forgotten that I'd had nothing to eat since lunch time, and I realized I was ravenously hungry.

Genny and I dismounted as a young man with jet black braids walked toward us.

Genny gave me the sign for silence again, and turned to speak to the man. I can't tell you what they said, but they seemed to know each other and the conversation, while urgent, had a friendly tone. Genny turned and indicated that I should follow her. We walked to the edge of the fire where men sat on huge logs that formed a seating area across from the collection of longhouses. They made space for us, and we sat together. I was handed a wooden plate upon which rested some of the meat I had smelled cooking earlier, along with what looked like a piece of flat bread. Not exactly crisp-chewy chocolate chip cookies, but I was starving and would have eaten dirt by now. I dove in, all feelings of guilt that Marley wasn't sharing this meal buried by reason; I'd search better on a full stomach.

As I wolfed down the food I noticed several of the younger men gathering horses. As soon as I finished, Genny filled me in on the plan, and all too soon we were back on the mare, following the group away from the camp.

This ride was not only shorter, it was at a much smoother pace, and by now I was feeling like Daniel Boone or maybe even Buffalo Bill. I'm sure Genny was grateful that I hadn't had to put the death grip into use on this trip. My confidence was short-lived, however, when I realized we were dismounting again, somehow knowing that we were about to enter the danger zone.

Genny linked her arm through mine and instantly I felt relief flood through me. It was such a Marley thing to do, and I could have hugged Genny at that moment; that is, if I weren't a twelve year-old boy. We followed Genny's native friends, who moved like tigers on the hunt, until we came to the garrison that had once been Genny's home. We crept around to the front, careful not to alert the tower guards, and stopped.

Genny was right so far; there was no one lurking about. Then, as if on cue, a rumbling, rattling sound came toward us from somewhere off in the night. It had to be Cyrus; nobody in their right mind would be wandering around the woods at this hour, far from the safety of the stockade walls. Sure enough, the enormous black stallion came into view, pulling the wagon that had been loaded in the barn. Fearing I might turn superhero at the sight, Genny held her arm out in front of me as her friends approached the wagon. I was happy to sit tight for now, waiting for what would surely be a bloody fight as the natives met the Englishmen.

To my astonishment the men greeted each other warmly. As they exchanged words, I tried to make sense of what was going on. Even Genny looked confused when her friends turned toward the woods without giving us a backward glance, the wagon following behind. They had simply left us standing where we were! As quickly and quietly as we could, Genny and I hustled back to our horse and threw ourselves up into the saddle. She led the horse around the back of the garrison just in time to catch a glimpse of the party receding into the woods. Luckily the wagon and horses made enough noise that we could fall in behind without being detected, and the darkness provided perfect cover. Neither of us said a word as we rode behind the natives and the gun runners and Marley.

Chapter 10

The wagon team couldn't travel through the woods as quickly as we could on horseback alone, so the trip back to the native village seemed to take forever; I half expected to see the sun coming up soon. My anxiety was made worse by the fact that even Genny seemed uncertain of what would happen next, and my hopes of this ordeal ever ending was fading with the night. The sedate trotting of the mare and a full stomach were all I was grateful for at the moment.

At last we reached the edge of the clearing, where we remained, along with the man Genny had spoken with earlier. He had circled back through the woods as we traveled, and it was apparent that Genny trusted him as they exchanged words briefly. We watched, I somewhat hopelessly, as the wagon stopped and Cyrus disembarked from the buckboard and approached the men gathered around the fire. He spoke directly to the man who looked to be the leader, and then they walked a short distance, entering the largest longhouse.

From our place in the tree line, Genny whispered to me that Cyrus was bargaining with the native leader, and that her friends had a plan to rescue Marley, but that we needed to be patient. "What the heck", I thought, "what's another couple of hours in the 17th century?" Just as long as I didn't have to spend much more time on this horse, that is; it was getting a little crowded in the saddle, and my legs were starting to go numb.

I'm not sure when, but the young man who had been waiting with us had disappeared. Hoping this wasn't a bad omen, I returned my gaze to the wagon, wanting to keep an eye on Marley in case this fiasco took another turn for the worse. I was worried that if we didn't rescue her from her coffin soon, she'd run out of air and die right in front of me.

Despite Genny's plea for patience, I knew we were running out of time, and I began to work on a plan to free Marley. I had no idea what the natives had planned, and I sure didn't want to get into hot water with them, but this was a desperate situation.

The man who had accompanied Cyrus was sitting on a log, lost in the feast the natives had provided him, which meant the wagon was unattended. It was parked just beyond the group around the fire, with the back end toward the woods, out of view. I figured I could make my way to the wagon without being detected, but I had no idea how I could pry the lid off without creating a major ruckus. I could crawl up into the back and try to talk to Marley, but I was pretty sure it would take more than a whisper to penetrate the pine box that imprisoned her. No matter how hard I tried, I just couldn't figure a way to free her by myself. My only choice was to trust these people who were 400 years older than I, and complete strangers to me until tonight at that.

As despair descended over me like a shroud, I was jolted into reality when Cyrus and the native leader emerged from the longhouse. Cyrus' partner rose from his log, and the three men walked to the wagon. I held my breath as the Indian inspected the shipment. Beside me I heard Genny's sharp intake of breath and, when I turned to her, I saw contempt and anger on her face, even as she uttered but one word.

"Papa."

"Papa?" I whispered in shock. "One of them is your papa?"

"Aye!" she whispered in a hiss. "Cyrus is my papa's business partner. They are traders here, providing supplies to the garrison. And I am certain they trade guns to the natives on the side, which they will then use to slaughter any who try to cheat or harm them. To him it is just business, but my friends and I fear that one day a terrible war may break out. There have been incidents already, and there is great tension."

"Whoa!" I exclaimed, realizing now the reason for the tunnels as well Genny's anger. "No wonder everyone is so friendly with each other! The natives are trying to protect themselves from being cheated by the Englishmen, and your papa just sees the natives as a bigger market for his business, using the tunnels to keep it a secret from the rest of the colony. Intense!"

Before I knew what was happening, Genny kicked the mare into motion and we bolted into the clearing. I nearly toppled from my place behind her, having no warning of what she was planning to do, and grabbed onto her just in time. The horse covered the distance in seconds and Genny brought her to a skidding halt that threatened to send us both headlong into the dirt, right at her father's feet. These near-death experiences were shortening my life span considerably and I figured I'd have aged enough to be playing for the Red Sox by the time we got back to the 21st century. Maybe by then my mother will have perfected her cookie baking skills.

"Genevieve Parker!" her father bellowed. "What are you doing here in the middle of the night. And with this… this…BOY!?"

"And you, papa, what are you doing here, trading guns to my friends when all they want is to be left in peace?" Genny shot back accusingly.

"Speak not of that which you know nothing of." her father warned.

"I know that you bring guns here, papa, and while I'm sure you see it as business, there is a greater price to be paid when the land flows with blood." Genny retorted scornfully.

"Silence!" Jonas Parker demanded. "I will deal with you when I am finished here. You will return to the wagon and wait." he ordered, but Genny held her ground and kept her seat on the mare, glaring at her father.

"As for you, boy, what business have you with my daughter?"

"I--I--I." I stammered, looking to Genny for help explaining my presence. When none came, I continued, "I have no idea, sir."

My helpless response took him by surprise and the anger in his eyes seemed to soften slightly. The mere thought of having to tell my bizarre tale again was draining me of whatever energy I had left. I might as well just order up my own pine box and cozy up next to Marley in the wagon, so spent was I after this endlessly outlandish night. My shoulders sagged and I began to slip from my perch in the saddle. I felt myself falling and braced myself for a hard landing. Instead, I landed in the arms of Genny's young friend, who then placed me on my feet. My knees buckled, but I managed to remain upright.

At that moment, the Indian leader approached Genny, holding out his hand in a gesture indicating he would help her dismount. After hesitating, Genny relented to his silent request, standing stubbornly between me and her friend. The leader then walked back toward the fire, apparently expecting us to follow his lead. The others who had been occupying the logs had vanished, so we had the area to ourselves. The men sat on one log while we younger ones sat on another. This scene looked like it might take a while to play out, and my thoughts returned to poor Marley. I couldn't wait any longer.

"Please, sir. You have my friend in a coffin in the back of your wagon. Could you please get her out before she dies in there?" I begged desperately.

"Your friend? The girl we found in the tunnel is with you?" was Jonas Parker's incredulous reply. "Aye, she is dressed in the same strange clothing you wear. Cyrus, bring the girl here."

"Thank you, sir, thank you so much!" I breathed, letting out a sigh of relief so enormous that I thought I might blow the fire out.

Cyrus left and within minutes he returned, carrying a limp Marley in his arms. I leapt from my seat and ran to her, certain as soon as I saw her that I had both found and lost her in the same moment. Her eyes were closed and even in the firelight she looked pale as death.

A litter was produced and Cyrus laid Marley on it, covering her with a blanket that had also appeared. The Indian leader spoke to the younger man who headed toward a teepee. In a flash he was back, accompanied by a very thin old man with long gray hair and leathery, wrinkled skin. He knelt next to Marley and began chanting some strange words in a sing-song voice. He placed some thick, dark, foul-smelling paste on Marley's forehead and continued chanting, but Marley didn't move a muscle. She's gone, I thought. My best friend is gone.

Chapter 11

I didn't care who saw me or what they thought. Huge tears rolled down my cheeks as I finally succumbed to the events of this long, hideous night. Losing the game was nothing compared to what was happening to me now. My shoulders heaved as I sobbed helplessly, inconsolable over the loss of my friend. Finally my tears were spent and my sobs slowed to hiccupping shudders of utter dejection. My head hung between my knees as I collapsed into myself. I felt Genny's arm around my shoulder, but I couldn't look at her just now. I no longer cared about returning to Marble Manor if I had to go without my best friend.

When I was finally able to lift my head, the first thing I saw was Genny's huge smile.

How could she possibly be smiling at me, I thought, enraged by grief. There was absolutely nothing to be so ridiculously happy about, which I was about to tell her, when she spoke to me.

"Master Jake, your friend is alive!" she exclaimed joyously. "Come, she is asking for you."

"Alive? Asking for me? Impossible!" I yelled. She hadn't moved, not even a twitch, all the while the old man had chanted over her and slathered her forehead with gunk that made a skunk smell like roses.

"It's true," vowed Genny. "Come and see for yourself!"

She led me to the place where Marley lay, and as afraid as I was to look at her still, pale face, I forced my eyes downward.

Incredibly, I saw a pair of clear, summer-sky blue eyes staring up at me, a mixture of confusion, fear, and relief playing over her face. I let out a wild whoop of joy, dropping to my knees to be closer to my resurrected friend.

"Welcome back, Mar." I said reverently, still amazed that she had rejoined me. "I thought you were gone for sure."

"So did I, Jake," she whispered back. "I was sure I'd never see you again when those men found me in the tunnel."

"Do you feel like you can sit up?" I asked. "Yeah, if you can help me up," she answered.

I helped Marley get slowly to her feet, and with her arm over my shoulder and mine around her waist, I walked her over to the log where Genny and I had been sitting.

Genny appeared, bringing with her a plate of food and mug of water for Marley. Once she had eaten and taken a long drink of water, I brought Marley up to speed on what had been happening on my end, introducing her to Genny. She remained silent as I told her all that had gone on, staring in awe when she discovered who Genny was and where we were.

Then it was her turn to tell us what had happened to her once we split up in the tunnel.

She had had the misfortune to be directly under the trap door when Cyrus opened it, apparently on his way to making this latest shipment of guns. He had leapt into the passageway and grabbed her, hauling her back the way we had come, but not through the closet! When Marley had reached the end of her tunnel, there was another trap door directly above, leading to the kitchen. This is where she and Cyrus had reentered the house. The man we now knew as Jonas Parker was there, waiting for Cyrus to arrive.

They hadn't planned to find a strange girl in the tunnel and now had no idea what to do with her. Not wanting to leave her alone in the house, they brought her into the barn and placed her in the crate.

We had been so engrossed in sharing our stories that we hadn't given a thought to the men who had abducted her, and I turned toward them now, feeling the seeds of outrage building inside me. These men were traitors, profiteers, and kidnappers, and at that moment, I wanted to see them hang. Genny sat with us still, but her friend had joined the men at some point. Genny, too, looked like she might be capable of murdering her own father and quite possibly her friend. The two of us sat there, seething, while Marley rested after finishing her harrowing tale. We needed a plan, any plan, to bring this night to an end.

At almost the same moment, the men turned our way. Genny's friend crossed the distance between us, and spoke quietly to Genny. I watched as the anger written on her face changed to confusion, and then doubt. Her friend's words became more urgent, almost pleading, in tone, and Genny's face softened slightly then as she gave him a nod.

"He asks that we join them and listen to their story." she explained, with a trace of contempt in her voice. The three of us rose, and made our way slowly toward the group. From the look on Genny's face, I doubted that she wanted to be anywhere near her father, but somehow her friend had convinced her to make the move. We sat across from the natives, Cyrus, and Jonas Parker, waiting expectantly for what they would tell us.

The Indian leader spoke first, in halting but clear English, to our astonishment! "Young ones, you have been brave. You have endured much and are strong.

Listen now to my words and believe what I tell you, for it is all true."

"Genevieve, you have my son's respect and friendship, and I honor you. Your heart is strong and true, and you are a friend to all my people. But you must know that your father is also our friend and a good man of honor. He does not trade to grow rich. We have made a pact to end bloodshed between our people."

The look on Genny's face ranged from anger, to doubt, to shocked surprise. She looked at her father as though meeting him for the first time. The look he returned to her was gentle and filled with subtle hope.

"For many months we have worked together to take guns meant to be used in war, hiding them until your father could find a way to trade them back. He would pick up the guns in the port when the ships arrived, and hide them in the tunnels beneath your land.

Late at night he would then bring them here, to a secret place, where my people switched the crates. When it was time, your father would return to pick them up and deliver them back to the ship, disguised as crates of grain and seed."

By now we all felt not only relief, but even a little ashamed for thinking such sinister thoughts. The chief continued his story.

"So, Genevieve, your father and Cyrus are traitors, as you say. They refuse to slaughter my people to gain more land and riches for England. They have the support of most of your people, but there are a few greedy men who wish to control all they survey. At great risk, your father and Cyrus work to keep peace. We have joined with them in a pact to help each other live in peace and prosperity."

When the chief had finished, Genny leapt from the log and ran to her father where he stood, waiting with open arms.

"Oh, papa!" she cried. "I am ashamed and not worthy to be your daughter. After mama died, you were gone so much and so stern. You moved at night in secret, and I was certain you were doing something awful. I knew of the tunnels and would sometimes listen as you and Cyrus talked. When I followed you one night and saw what you were doing, I had to tell someone, so sure was I of your guilt. I am terribly sorry."

"Hush, my daughter. I knew of your friendship and was happy for you. I know you have been lonely with your mama gone and me so busy. But when I discovered you missing I feared for your safety. If men from the garrison found you, or learned about my deceit, you would have been in grave danger. I locked you in the shed to keep you safe, my dear. I could not bear it if anything happened to my sweet girl."

Genny's father held his daughter and quieted her sobs, assuring her of his love for her.

Then he turned to Marley and me and said, "Now, what are we to do about the two of you?"

Chapter 12

That was a good question, I thought. Now that everything had settled down, the focus was back on Marley and me, and I was certainly clueless as to how we would go about returning to our place and time. I was also pretty sure none of these people had any experience in time travel either, so the situation was looking pretty grim.

"Let us return to our home, and then we will discuss what is to be done. We will travel through the woods to avoid drawing attention to our party." decided Genny's father.

We said our good-byes and thank you to the natives, and piled into the wagon, this time sitting atop Marley's former coffin, arms linked once again. The comfort of that familiar gesture calmed me and I actually smiled for the first time in hours. Genny's mare was tethered to the back of the wagon, and we slowly moved into the deep woods once again. This time the trip didn't seem as terrifying as we headed toward familiar territory. We disembarked at the front of the house while Cyrus was instructed to tend to the horses and wagon.

The first threads of daylight appeared in the dark sky, lending a soft light to the night that was about to leave us. Now we could see the porch, which spanned the front of the house, giving it a welcoming look. It made me sad to think that this porch had not withstood the test of time, a fact only Marley and I were aware of just then. We trouped up the steps and into the house, winding through the foyer and the living room,ending up in the kitchen. Lanterns were lit and we took our seats at the table.

"Please, young ones share your tale with me now, so that we may determine how to resolve this strange predicament." was Jonas Parker's request.

Once again I related the events of the night, sticking to the main points and assisted this time by Marley. As we wound our way through all that had happened, I felt my bones grow heavier, weighing me down with exhaustion so complete I feared I would fall asleep in the middle of the telling. Once the story was done, silence descended upon us all as Genny's father considered all he had learned. Just as I was about to nod off, a familiar punch startled back to reality.

"Jake!" Marley squealed. "I forgot all about the letters and the diary. Do you still have them?"

"Of course I do." I replied grumpily as I rubbed my shoulder. I reached behind me and placed the pile of papers on the wooden table.

Genny gasped softly as she reached for the packets of letters. She drew them to her and held them to her heart, tears shining in her eyes. Her father looked on gently, his own eyes brimming with tears.

"These are letters mama and papa wrote to each other after papa first came here. He was here for nearly a year before he returned to England to fetch us. They are all I have left of mama and I am grateful you are returning them to me."

Then Genny slowly slid her diary toward her, embarrassed that we might have been privy to her most personal thoughts and feelings.

"We never read the letters or your diary Genny." Marley softly reassured her. "We found them in the bedrooms, and took them thinking that they might help us find our way back home. We are happy to return them to you. And here is a notebook we found, Mr. Parker." said Marley as she handed it to him.

"Well, Mar." I said, "That's not exactly true." Now it was my turn to be embarrassed. "We did read that one diary page we found in the crypt, and that's when this whole crazy adventure began."

"But how is it that you come from a different time and yet are in possession of my daughter's papers?" queried a skeptical Jonas Parker. "You are dressed in an odd manner, but to travel back 400 years in time can not be possible. Perhaps you are spies for the greedy men who wish to ruin our peace."

"Mr. Parker, we have no idea who you are speaking of and we have no idea how we got here other than the story we told you. Where we are from it is now 2006, and we have many conveniences you have never heard of." I explained.

"He's right!" added Marley eagerly. "We have hot and cold running water in our homes, electric lights that we turn on and off with a switch, televisions, and microwave ovens that can cook food in minutes!"

Jonas Parker looked completely bewildered, and Marley and I might as well have been Martians from outer space, so foreign were these ideas to the Parkers. Suddenly I had an idea. I leaned over and whispered to Marley, only later apologizing for my rudeness.

Marley nodded her head, eyes shining with excitement. She reached into her pocket and brought her hand out slowly, realizing that Jonas Parker peered at her with a mixture of fear and doubt written on his brow.

"Mr. Parker, you are familiar with coins, I'm sure?" I asked. "Of course." he replied indignantly.

"Then you will recognize that what Marley is about to hand you is a coin. It may look different in color, value, and markings, but it is a coin of legal tender. On the face you will see George Washington, first president of the United States of America. In about 150 years the Revolutionary War will be fought in order for twelve colonies to gain their independence from England. George Washington was a great general in this war, and he was later elected president of the new country. I ask that you please look at it, and note the date when you do."

Marley handed the coin to Jonas Parker, and Genny looked over his shoulder with interest. He turned the coin over in his hand, looking at each side carefully. He even placed it between his teeth and bit down to be certain it was real. Then he looked up at us, his face registering confusion and awe.

"Master Jake, what you say is true." he said quietly. "While I am mystified as to how this has occurred, I can see the date is 1998, and the coin indeed proves you live far into the future from where we now sit."

He then held the coin out to me, but I declined, saying, "Please keep it so that you will still have proof even after Marley and I make it back to our world. If we make it back."

He placed the coin into his pocket, and then returned his gaze to mine, asking, "Do you still have that page from Genny's diary as well?" sounding hopeful and almost excited.

"It's right here." I said as I pulled the slightly crumpled sheet from my back pocket.

"Since this paper seems to be the link between your time and ours, perhaps it will also provide a way back through for you." he proposed. "Where did you say you first found yourselves when you awoke?"

"In the shed." we replied in unison.

"Then perhaps we should return and see if the answer somehow lies there." Mr. Parker said decisively as he rose from his chair. "Genny, bring your diary but leave the letters here. Don't look so fearful my daughter, I won't read your secret thoughts." he said more gently, reading the look on his daughter's face.

Genny's shoulders dropped back into position as she released the breath she'd been holding. She smiled at her father, and it was obvious the two of them loved each other very much. That exchange made me long to be back in my own home with my mom, pop, and even my little sister.

Mr. Parker picked up a lantern, patted me on the shoulder, and slowly herded us toward the back door. The sky had turned a soft pink as dawn birthed a new day, and after we had descended the steps, we linked arms. But this time, there were three of us, connected to each other forever by this bizarre odyssey. We drew strength from and gave comfort to each other as we crossed the dewy grass, arriving at the shed as birdsong replaced the night sounds. After one last reassuring squeeze, we broke the link and slipped one by one into the shed.

Genny placed her diary on the table as we stood in a semi-circle around it. I handed the missing page to Marley, figuring it was a girl thing. Somehow then we knew that another journey was about to begin, and we had to part with Genny and her father.

Recalling the dates in the crypt, a deep sadness overcame me when I realized how little time Genny had left, and how bereft her father would be without her.

"I-I-I guess this means good-bye." I stammered.

"I have been glad to know you, Jake and Marley, and I will miss you both. Thank you for bringing papa and I back together again." Genny whispered as tears spilled onto her cheeks.

"You have done much for us, young Jake and Marley." Jonas Parker solemnly spoke, bowing slightly in our direction. "I wish you safe travels back to where you belong."

I couldn't speak at that moment for fear my voice would fail me completely or come out as a squeak, so I turned to Marley. Her own cheeks showed a trail of tears as she moved toward Genny and gave her a hug. No words were exchanged between the girls, the contact itself speaking volumes instead. Finally the embrace ended and Marley returned to my side.

"Return to the spot where you first passed through." instructed Mr. Parker as he moved to his daughter's side. He placed his arm around her shoulders as hers encircled his waist.

"Genny, open the diary to the place where the missing page should be." he said.

Genny did as he asked, and then he turned to us one final time. "Marley, give Genny the page, please."

Marley gazed down at the beautiful handwriting once more, before handing the page to Genny with reverence, knowing this crumpled and yellowed page was a sacred artifact that held incredible power. The air around us felt at once stifling and electric.

"Are you ready?" Mr. Parker asked.

Marley and I linked arms and nodded that we were.

"Very well; Genevieve, insert the page back where it belongs, and close the book please."

Marley and I exchanged a glance, linking our arms even tighter in preparation for what we dearly hoped would be the next and final leg of our amazing sojourn. Genny carefully inserted the page back into her diary. As she slowly closed the book, she raised her hand in a wave, and the swirling darkness swallowed us once again.

Chapter 13

My cheek was cold and damp where I lay on the floor, and the sulfury odor of an electrical storm lingered in the air. I saw a small flickering light in the darkness, as next to me Marley moaned softly. Once my eyes had adjusted to the gloom I arose cautiously, making sure nothing was broken then bent to help Marley to her feet. I felt a small shudder course through her as she stood.

Not entirely sure what had happened, and perhaps too spooked to speak, we just stood there reading the look of uncertainty in each others eyes. Marley was the first to break the silence.

"Jake, where are we?" she asked, nervously, as if dreading my answer.

"Uh, we're still in the crypt, Mar." I said, not ready to admit aloud what I thought had happened to us.

Thud.

"Geez, Mar, how much more do you think this arm can take? I'd like to finish the season in one piece, if you don't mind!" I hollered, my voice reverberating in the small space. I was instantly sorry for bellowing because my poor ears were ringing like church bells all over again.

"Then why don't you stop giving me useless answers and enlighten me, Jake, because I'd like to know exactly what went on here." Marley replied stubbornly.

Knowing her squeaks would lead to shrieks, but not sure where to begin, I cautiously floated a question her way.

"Mar, how many candles do you see over by the bench?" Marley turned to look and let out a startled gasp.

"One!" came the answer.

"Then it must be true." I whispered, awe-struck, "because I am sure there were two there when we came in. Do you see the crumpled paper anywhere?"

We both spent a minute looking corner to corner, searching the floor, but to no avail.

The crypt was empty save for us and one candle, flickering in its red glass chimney. Marley stooped to pick up the candle, leading led the way to Genevieve Parker's tomb. She held the candle aloft, and we both sucked in a huge gulp of the cool, dank air.

There on the tomb were the dates of Genevieve's birth and death. Just as before, her date of birth still read 24 August 1605. But the date of her death was no longer 27 September 1619. Judging from the date we read there now, Genny had grown up and lived far past the fourteen years we had thought, for now it read 19 July 1649!

"19 July! The same date as the page from her diary." Marley breathed in wonder. "She lived another 30 years after we met her! Maybe the work her father and the natives did actually saved her life."

"Mar, I don't know about you, but this has been the spookiest night of my entire life, and all I want to do now is go home." I pleaded, feeling as though I would drop from shock and exhaustion where I stood. "We can get together tomorrow and figure this out. My brain can't take any more right now."

"You're right, Jake." agreed Marley worriedly. "It's too much for my brain too, and if we don't get home soon, there will be search parties dredging the river."

Slowly I eased the crypt door open as Marley replaced the candle. Somehow we had come to a silent agreement that we wanted to leave this place and its contents behind us for now. The rain had stopped, except for the "tree rain" that splattered us in short bursts as the wind rustled through branches.

Amazingly, no time seemed to have passed as we hurried through the final wisps of the misty dusk, emerging onto the tree-lined lanes of Marble Manor, where street lights cast a comforting glow. We arrived at Marley's house first, where lamplight welcomed her home and the front porch was thankfully intact. We walked up the front walk, where the daffodils bowed their sunny heads in slumber, then up the steps, stopping just outside the door.

"Okay Mar, we made it safely. But tomorrow we seriously need to meet, preferably in a nice sunny spot, and try to make sense out of what happened to us tonight." I said soberly.

Marley nodded and suggested we meet in the park. We decided on the bench near the fountain pool, where water streamed endlessly from the mouth of a marble fish held by a boy doomed never to splash in its cool depths. In other words, a nice, normal place where we could discuss the extraordinary adventure we had shared. We agreed noon would be perfect, and I offered to bring the chips and soda, while Marley chose to bring the PB&J sandwiches. Just talking about doing something so ordinary made me feel better.

Before I left her to return to my house, we linked arms one last time, then took a solemn vow to never, ever, as long as we lived, cross our hearts and hope to die, stick a needle in our eye, tell another living breathing soul about what happened that night at Shady Lawn. But apparently Marley wasn't satisfied with our usual pledge, so just for good measure she landed a final blow to my arm before darting through the front door, grinning like a ghoul.

I walked next door, then up the driveway, rubbing my bruised and swollen arm, and rounded the back of my house. I trudged up the back steps, stopping to remove my muddy cleats. Mostly I don't need to listen to my mother, being the brilliant twelve year old boy that I am, but I knew my arm couldn't possibly take having to sweep and mop the kitchen floor if I tracked in a mess.

I peered through the window in the door, and there was my mother, scooping cookie dough onto metal sheets. I raised my eyes skyward in a silent prayer that maybe, just maybe, this time she'd get them crisp-chewy perfect. My pop sat at the kitchen table, with a tall glass of milk in front of him, listening to the Red Sox on the radio as he waited to gobble cookies warm from the oven. Suddenly I didn't care how the cookies turned out, or that my pop would launch into a full game analysis the second I stepped in the room. In fact, I no longer cared that I had lost the game.

Never before had I been so happy to be home. Never before had I so madly wanted to devour as many chocolate chip cookies as I could without puking. Never before did I need a hug from my mother as desperately as I did at that moment.

I flung open the door and melted into the comforting safety, the reassuring warmth, and the divine aroma of my home.

THE END...